TEA . . . AND SYMPATHY

She broke off, and then asked abruptly, "Was it you who sat her up against the pillows?"

"Indeed not," I replied. "I didn't touch her."

"Funny—Mrs. Deane says she didn't either. Oh, Lord. I don't know . . . Looks as though we're all in it together."

"What on earth do you mean, Nurse?" I demanded indignantly.

"She was all right when I went out," she said obstinately, "and now she's dead . . . Give me some more sugar in this, it tastes frightful. I like Indian tea really, not this sick-making China muck."

"Well, I'll make you another pot," I suggested.

"No go dear. My Indian tea's in her room, and the room's locked up as I told you." She added, thoughtfully: "She won't have any further need for that precious tea of hers in the antique caddy—will she?"

—from *NO FLOWERS BY REQUEST*

CRIME ON THE COAST

by
JOHN DICKSON CARR,
VALERIE WHITE,
LAURENCE MEYNELL,
JOAN FLEMING,
MICHAEL CRONIN,
ELIZABETH FERRARS

&

NO FLOWERS BY REQUEST

by
DOROTHY L. SAYERS,
E. C. R. LORAC,
GLADYS MITCHELL,
ANTHONY GILBERT,
CHRISTIANNA BRAND

BERKLEY BOOKS, NEW YORK

CRIME ON THE COAST and NO FLOWERS BY REQUEST

A Berkley Book/published by arrangement with the authors' estates

PRINTING HISTORY
Victor Gollancz edition published 1984
Berkley edition/November 1987

ISBN: 0-425-10417-6

A BERKLEY BOOK® TM 757,375
Berkley Books are published by The Berkley Publishing Group,
200 Madison Avenue, New York, NY 10016.
The name "BERKLEY" and the "B" logo
are trademarks belonging to Berkley Publishing Corporation.

PRINTED IN THE UNITED STATES OF AMERICA

10 9 8 7 6 5 4 3 2 1

CONTENTS

CRIME ON THE COAST

NO FLOWERS BY REQUEST   73

CRIME ON THE COAST

I

THE FUN FAIR

John Dickson Carr

HE DIDN'T LIKE August Bank Holidays. He didn't like crowded seaside resorts. When you combined the two of them, on the promenade at Breston where, this afternoon, the whole South of England seemed to be shouting in his ear—he felt he was getting his money's worth of gloom.

"Adventure!" he said aloud, with a disgusted flourish. "Adventure, my eye! Nuts and double nuts!"

Phil Courtney was not really a stuffed shirt. On the contrary, all fifty thousand of the passers-by would have seen a personable young man in his early thirties. But he felt like that, and he said so.

Head down, under a hot sky curdling to grey and with prowling thunder off the sea, he pushed through the uproar of the Fun Fair at the western end of the promenade. Blaring music from a merry-go-round was drowned in the roar of a diving switch-back. Toy balloons, red and yellow and blue, popped and disappeared as some humorist used a lighted cigarette.

This pleased Phil, who beamed with approval on the cursing balloon-vendor.

"What's more," he continued, as dust stung his eyes in the rising wind, "in about two minutes it's going to bucket with rain. That will complete the gaiety of nations. That will—"

"Wotchersay, chum?" inquired a voice in his ear.

Phil jumped and woke up. A crash of thunder, drawing squeals from the crowd and making it ripple, found him staring into the eyes of a fat bowler-hatted man who had been shouting the attractions of an ornate cavern called Ye Olde Haunted Mill.

"Wotchersay, chum?"

Phil assumed his most oratorical air.

"My friend," he said, "did you ever make a bet?"

"Cor!" said the fat man, and shivered and shut his eyes. "Did I ever make a *bet*!"

"I did not refer," said Phil, with as grand a gesture as though he had never dropped a packet himself, "to a bet on a horse. Did some treacherous friend of yours, for instance, ever bet you that you would find material for a story—"

"Wot story?"

"Any story! A story to write! I write. Did some treacherous friend, I repeat, ever bet you that you would find the true stuff of adventure, the rich pang of human interest, if only you spent two weeks in a howling inferno like this town?"

"Oh, ah. Adventure." The fat man's eye strayed to a neat brunette in slacks and a halter. "There's plenty of 'em, chum," he said.

"Yes; but I didn't exactly mean that."

"The old 'aunted mill!" bellowed the fat man,

suddenly remembering his duties. "You!" He pointed in Phil's face. "Take a luverly ride in a boat through the old 'aunted mill!"

Phil Courtney was again exasperated.

"Now wouldn't I look damn silly sitting alone in one of those little boats-for-two, and floating through the dark with a lot of fake ghosts and skeletons? That's the sort of place where you take your girl, and I don't know a soul in this—"

"*Phil! My dear!*" said a girl's voice just behind him.

She spoke breathlessly, her hand on his shoulder, and with the air of one who was something more than a friend. She was fair-haired and grey-eyed, all in white, with a quickened breathing and a heightened colour. She was so attractive that, even at first glance, it made his head sing.

And he had never seen her before in his life.

"I was terribly afraid I'd lost you, Phil," she went on in that quick, slurred, nervous voice. "And I did so want to visit the—the old haunted mill. Won't you take me in with you?"

Then she added, with desperate entreaty but in so low a voice that he hardly heard her:

"Please! It's a matter of life and death!"

Another shock of thunder struck close, and the storm tore down. Instantly the whole area near them was swept as clean of people as though somebody had cut loose with a machine-gun. Phil and the grey-eyed girl stood looking at each other in the thickening rain, paying no attention to it.

"Nothing would please me better," he said sincerely, "than to escort you through the old haunted mill. Come on."

He thrust money through the window of a pay-box, and handed two tickets to the fat man. All this time, while the rain drove in their faces, the girl kept glancing over her shoulder and gripping her handbag in an agony of apprehension.

"Hurry!" she urged. "Please hurry!"

"Yes, I know. This rain is the devil."

"Oh, not the rain. That's wonderful! That helps with everything!"

"Madam," said Phil, "you take a more tolerant view of the climate than anybody I ever met. As for helping with everything—"

"But don't you see? There's nobody near us, and I ought to be able to tell if anybody is following me. Wait!"

She looked at the fat man, who was pushing out a cockleshell wooden boat into a channel of softly running water just wide enough to let it slip through. Opening her handbag, the girl drew out two rather large snapshots.

"Will you take these two photographs," she said to the fat man, "and keep them for me until I get out?"

"*Wot?*"

"Oh, I know it sounds mad! But it isn't. I swear it isn't! Look at the photographs, please!"

The fat man, who clearly regarded both Phil and the girl as a pair of loonies eminently suited to each other, nevertheless did as he was asked.

"Would you recognize either of those two men if you saw them here? Would you?"

"Dunno, Miss. I expect so. But—"

"Well!" said the girl. "If either of these two men

comes near here, or—or asks you questions about me, will you tell me when I come out?"

"Oi! Miss! I—"

A leap of lightning, followed by a tumbling explosion of thunder, stirred along Phil's nerves and made the two faces in the snapshots seem to open their eyes at him. One was an elderly, prosperous, cleft-chinned face, respectable to the point of starchiness. The other was a young man, clearly some relation to the first, with the same cleft-chinned good looks.

Both faces wore broad and fixed grins, like figures in a nightmare.

And Phil Courtney stepped straight into the Arabian Nights.

"Do as this lady asks you," he said, pressing a pound note into the fat man's hand, "and there'll be another of these for you afterwards. Into the boat, now!"

The boat, just wide enough for them to sit side by side, rocked and splashed underfoot. The fat man, muttering wildly under his breath, gave it a shove. And they drifted off into a damp tunnel of pitch darkness.

Now there was only a splashing, a whispering, a chuckling of water. Phil's voice echoed back at him, and he lowered it.

"Look here," he said. "I don't want to seem inquisitive, but hadn't you better tell me what this is all about?"

The girl gave a gasp that attempted to be a laugh. He could feel her arm trembling against his side.

"I'm sorry, Mr Courtney. You are Philip Courtney, aren't you?"

"Yes, that's right. But I've never met you before so help me! Or I couldn't have forgotten it."

"That's awfully nice of you, Mr Courtney."

" 'Mr Courtney?' A minute ago . . ."

"Please! I couldn't help myself! I had to go to somebody, and I thought I could trust you. You don't know me, but I know you. At least, I know of you. I'm a friend of Mr Westlake."

"Jimmy Westlake? The bloated publisher who bet me I couldn't spend a week at the Royal Scarlet Hotel without finding . . . never mind. Go on."

"My name's Nita Ross. I—I read a lot of manuscripts for Mr Westlake. And I've seen you in the office, though I don't work there. Then, when I ran away from London this morning—"

"Why did you run away from London?"

"Well, you see," said Nita Ross, "twice in the past week somebody has tried to kill me."

II

INTO THE TUNNEL

John Dickson Carr

A SCREECH OF brassy laughter from some machine in the tunnel rang witch-like past the swaying boat. Both of them started, and Phil peered round at a quick-breathing girl he couldn't see.

"Just a minute. Is this a joke or something?"

"No! No! No!"

"Steady, now. Who tried to kill you?"

"I don't know, except that it must have been somebody in my own home. That's the worst of it, don't you see? Imagine you're in your own home, where you think everything is sane and comfortable . . ."

"Well?"

"And you walk out into the garden. And somebody laughs. And a stone flower-box, weighing eighty or a hundred pounds, comes crashing down from an upstairs window and just misses you. That flower-box would have crushed me to a pulp on the terrace."

"But couldn't it have been an accident?"

7

"Yes, that's what *they* said."

"Who said?"

"My Uncle Hubert and my Cousin Charles. It was Thursday afternoon, and the servants were out. Uncle Hubert and Cousin Charles were the only people in the house except my Aunt Marion: and she doesn't count."

Before Phil Courtney's eyes, in the dark, floated a vision of two faces: one old, one young, with cleft chins and fixed grins.

"Uncle Hubert and Cousin Charles? Those are the two men in the snapshots?"

"Yes. And *they* said it was an accident. They soothed me and were very sympathetic. But what happened last night wasn't an accident. I woke up in the middle of the night, horribly frightened without knowing why. And then, all of a sudden, a pair of hands closed round my neck in the dark."

Nita's voice went up.

"Amusing, wasn't it?" she cried. "A terribly funny joke. But I managed to scream just before the hands could strangle me. I screamed and screamed, and the hands let go. I heard somebody move, and a door close. And then, when I turned on the light, there was nobody there."

The little boat, carried along by the softly lapping water, bumped slightly in its channel. Ahead showed a dim gleam of bluish light. They were approaching one of the tableaux, wax figures set in recesses, which added joy to the haunted waterway.

"But look here!" protested Phil. "Why should one of your own family want to hurt you?"

"That's just it. There isn't any reason."

"No reason at all?"

"No! My parents are dead: I've lived with Uncle Hubert and Aunt Marion since I was ten years old. He's very well off, and so respectable it's positively painful. I haven't any money: there's nothing they want me to do, or keep me from doing. In their own way they're all very fond of me. I haven't lived there all these years without knowing that. Mr Courtney, somebody is trying to kill me. But why?"

"Well, what did your respected relatives say when this merry joker tried to strangle you?"

"They said I was having a nightmare and dreamed it. They just—grinned and grinned and grinned."

Ha-ha screeched the brassy laughter from the machine in the tunnel, jarring their nerves like a dentist's drill against a tooth.

"And today, you say, you ran away from London?"

"Yes. I packed a bag, and took the first train for Breston, and put up at the Royal Scarlet Hotel. Don't you understand? I wanted to see whether somebody would follow me. In all this Bank Holiday crowd, I thought, I couldn't possibly be in any danger. And, if somebody did follow me . . . Well, I should know who was trying to kill me."

"All right: what happened? Did anybody follow you?"

"Yes. All of them."

"All of them?"

"Oh, not really! I mean: when you're as terrified as I was, your imagination turns everything into the image of what you're afraid to see. A hotel commissionaire looked exactly like Uncle Hubert. A woman selling sweets looked exactly like Aunt Marion. Then, when a young spiv raised his hat to me, I thought it was Cousin Charles and I completely lost my head.

Once—can you believe this?—I even thought I saw Mr Westlake."

"Jimmy Westlake? Now wait a minute!"

Nita's breathless laugh turned into something like a sob.

"I'm s-sorry! I shouldn't have bored you with all this. You don't believe me either. You think I'm hysterical or dreaming or making all this up!"

"My dear girl," said Phil, with his heart going out to her. "I don't think anything of the kind. But it did occur to me: if some lunatic really did follow you here . . ."

"Yes?"

"This dark tunnel would be a devil of a place to be trapped in."

The obvious trap is never the one we see in front of us. This, clearly, had never occurred to Nita: he felt her grow tense and rigid at his side, and he would have given anything to recall the words. But there was no recalling them now.

The soft slap-slap of the water, magnified in that damp enclosed space, seemed to beat in their ears. Very slowly they were moving past a recess, so dimly lighted that it was little more than a cave of shadows, in which the wax figure of a dead man lay on straw beside a ruined mill-wheel.

Then Nita's voice went piercing up:

"*Could* anybody follow us in here?"

"No! Forget what I said. It was only an idiotic idea from the lurid sort of fiction I write!"

"Don't try to humour me! Please don't try to humour me!—*Could* anybody?"

"To be practical about it, Nita, your merry joker

would have to come in a boat. And you don't see any boat behind us, do you?''

"No, but the water is only about eighteen inches deep. You could—you could wade through the water, couldn't you?''

"My dear Nita, your imagination is about ten times worse than mine. Why in the name of sense should anybody do that? Forget it, I tell you! There's not the least possibility—''

He paused abruptly, but it was a second or two before he realized why he had paused. It was because of the silence, and the lack of motion. There was no longer any sound of lapping water. And the boat had stopped, too.

It hung there, poised by the niche, with the dim bluish light shining on the waxen figure of the dead man, and on the pallor of Nita's face.

Very clearly, then, they both heard the next noise. Nita's head twitched round, and he saw her eyes shift and gleam as she glanced over her shoulder. But she spoke almost calmly

"You may think it's impossible,'' she said. "But there *is* somebody here with us.''

III

A BLOW IN THE DARK

Valerie White

PHIL LISTENED. SILENCE, as precarious and intense as when a great conductor first lifts his baton, clung about them, agonizingly prolonged. Then, he heard it again.

There could have been a variety of causes; yet, never for an instant did he have any doubt. Someone was wading through the shallow water. Whoever it might be was following in their tracks along the tunnel, stopping every now and then, perhaps to feel his way. Now he was near, very near indeed.

"Who's there?"

The shout burst from Phil in reflex before his mind had planned what to do. The echo swirled round them in their cave and ebbed away down the two sections of tunnel. It took Nita even more by surprise than himself. She was clutching his arm and her nails dug into the flesh of his wrist. A sob of undisguised terror told its own story.

Silence pressed down on them again. Now, there

13

was no whisper of movement, of legs swishing care-fully through shallow water.

Behind Nita, he could see the head of the wax figure lying beside its broken water-wheel. The male features, in green twilight, looked gangrenous and evil: the eyes were closed, as though they had seen all they had ever wished to see. And, nearer, beside him, the stranger: an unusually fair girl, with ner-vous hands and wide-set eyes, grey, and constantly on guard: on guard, standing sentinel to heaven knew what secret.

"This is ludicrous!"

"Why?"

"Why? Because it's Bank Holiday at Breston and we're alone in a Fun Fair tunnel."

"Alone? We're not. I know we're not."

Phil knew they were not too; but he refused to admit it again, even to himself. He laughed, but no one could have pretended that he sounded happy. Beside him, his free hand was trailing over the side of the boat. He was conscious that it was registering some sensation of urgent importance, but his mind would not concentrate on it.

Nita was clinging to his arm more fiercely than ever, tensed, listening.

"Why have we stopped?"

"How would I know? We must be jammed. There's probably something in this shallow water."

"I'm terrified. I know there's someone back there in that tunnel."

She was looking up at Phil as she spoke.

"Come on. Enough's enough. Let's get out of here and go back to the Royal Scarlet. We're letting our imaginations run away with us. Here: I'll try to shove us along with a hand on the wall. If that doesn't work, I'll paddle and push.''

With difficulty he disengaged his wrist. Nita was still very close to him.

"Oh, Phil! I did think you believed I was telling the truth.''

"Of course I believed you. It's merely that I now feel you may have been mistaken in what you believed to be true. Most of us are, most of the time.''

There was a wild, straining look about her now. It could have meant anything: hardly suppressed terror, a child's panic in keeping ahead of some creeping shadow of fear, a streak of insanity coming to the surface, anything.

Phil, looking at her, was reminded that sympathy towards a stranger, particularly towards a beautiful stranger, is most often no more than inquisitiveness. Well, if by nature he was inquisitive, he was certainly getting his money's worth this time.

On some hidden thought, she looked away from him. Her voice was no more than the echo of a whisper.

"Oh, how awful! Now I'm alone again, if you don't believe me.''

The appeal would have been as difficult to side-step as a flag-seller on Poppy Day, if he had wanted to do so. He did not.

He opened his mouth to make some suitably comforting reply. But no words came.

From behind them, down the tunnel, there sounded a creak as though a heavy, rusty wheel was being turned. But neither of them paid any attention. With a sudden start, she was almost on top of him.

Terror had pulled the skin tight across her face, her lips were drawn back from bared teeth and she was staring: staring at the ruined water-wheel.

Phil leant forward, the better to see.

The eyes of the figure stretched across its straw mattress were now half open.

For seconds, which strung themselves across what appeared to be an eternity of inertia, he watched, trying to probe the dim half-light. He was icy cold where he had been clammy hot. Then, blood began to flow in his veins again and his mind slipped back into gear.

"We're getting out of here! Now!"

It was a good idea. But, like a number of other good ideas, a trifle late.

Whatever hit him was hard and well aimed to the base of his skull. Leaning forward, his every attention on the prostrate figure, he presented a target fit for an amateur. In the event, he received professional treatment.

And, in that split second, as his head jerked forward, the message from his hand came through. The water was still: the current had ceased to flow. That then, and not more artificial means, had been the cause of their boat stopping. Under the circumstances, it was the day's least constructive thought.

It was still with him when he came to. "The current's not flowing . . . the current's not flowing . . . the current's not . . ." His mind returned to face the problem in hand only with reluctance. And, perhaps, with good reason for its reluctance.

He was stretched out, his hands clasped piously across his chest, beside the broken water-wheel. There was straw all around him: straw tickling his ears and pricking his ankles. Still, the dim green light shone. There was no sign of the wax figure whose place he had taken. Wax? His mind had been slow to recall those half-open eyes. There was no trace of the boat. His head was throbbing as though it housed a turbine.

There was a lump at the back, but no blood. His watch told him that it was a few minutes after five o'clock. He had been unconscious for the best part of an hour. It had, indeed, been a professional job.

Gritting his teeth in the pain of movement, he sat up. Off with his shoes and socks, his trousers rolled up above the knee and he was ready to move.

The water felt cold and the bottom slimy as he began to wade. All around him, hostile, nightmare darkness pressed down. He was still dazed and such reasoned thoughts as he could muster told him that he was scared: and, for the moment, perfectly prepared to admit it.

So selfish is the human mind in crisis. This was the first moment at which he gave a direct thought to Nita.

He wondered whether she too had been hit. If so, could she have survived a blow such as he had received? Or, perhaps, he had not been meant to survive either?

Rounding a bend, the channel widened again and darkness gave way to more thin green light. This time, the tableau was a slab of mill-stone. On it was stretched the figure of a girl, shrouded under a white sheet, her features drawn, ivory-glazed. Her eyes were closed. At her feet was set a huge stuffed owl.

The girl's nose reminded Phil of Nita's. Then he

saw that the chin was quite different. The eyes looked to him as though they were straining to open.

Phil knew he ought to climb out of the water and investigate. Without further delay he continued on his way.

Soon he was groping through pitch darkness again. Somewhere behind him an owl hooted.

IV

PHIL DROPS A BOMBSHELL

Valerie White

ROUND ONE LAST corner and Phil reached the open air. A clutter of little boats waiting for customers: two tunnel mouths: twenty-four-inch lettering proclaiming Ye Olde Haunted Mill; and, no fat, bowler hatted man wallowing in long rubber boots as he pushed the boats away.

No fat, bowler-hatted man; but, in his place, a vision of almost breath-taking beauty displayed with quite breathtaking abandon in and around a bikini.

"Excuse me. Is the man who saw me off still around anywhere? He's holding some photographs for me."

He had forgotten that he must appear a somewhat startling arrival from the tunnel: trousers rolled up, shoes in hand and boat lost without trace. The vision showed no inclination to overlook one facet of the joke. She laughed till she was even further out of her bathing dress.

"Sid? Sid's gone to fix the jets. Pumps packed in,

so it 'ad to be the emergencies. What about you? You been for a nice paddle, dear?"

"Hasn't Sid come out again though?"

"'Ere, what you want with Sid? What's 'is business to you, anyway? Any case, 'e's probably gone up through the pumps trap, by the ladder. 'Ere, mister, where's your boat?"

Trying to appear nonchalant whilst standing calf-deep in water surrounded by a Bank Holiday crowd is not easy. He failed.

"Have you seen a boat come out with only a girl in it? A very pretty girl, fair, grey eyes and . . ."

That was as much as he was allowed. The thunder had passed. The sun had re-emerged through a blur of rising steam, and a cataract of warm humanity had tumbled out of its sheltering places in search of further discomforts it could spend the remaining 364 days of the year trying to forget.

An over-garnished spiv, putting a price-tag on potential customers for a very special line of postcards, leant over the pool's railing and pointed a dirty fingernail.

" 'Ark at little Sir Galahad! Tipped yer aht, did she? Not a bad judge, neither, I'd say."

There was a roar of laughter, led by the girl in charge.

Phil started to explain. No one would listen. Then he lost his temper.

After he had attempted to arouse the interest of three separate policemen, his sense of proportion slowly returned. His story was incredible. He was plus one lump on the head and minus one girl-friend. What did it matter what he might say? The story told itself: especially on Bank Holiday. Even the police laughed, if in a kinder tone.

He put on his socks and shoes and began to walk along the Front, thinking.

Heavy, bruise-blue storm clouds swirled in the distance above terracotta villas poised on the headland across the bay. On this side, damp sunshine lit the rotten-green of an oily calm sea. As centrepiece, the Pier, a gaudy finger pointed towards France, barnacled with kiosks and cupolas. Linking it all, the Front itself represented a wide panorama of ill-planned abandon.

Not for the first time in his life, he was bemoaning to himself the limitations imposed by an expensive education which so ill-prepares its pupils for a life in which violence is a preliminary as opposed to a highly improbable aftermath to negotiation.

He paid at a turnstile and turned on to the Pier. Not far along, he discovered two benches set in a shallow recess and facing one another. On one there were three people, their faces hidden, busy reading newspapers. The other bench was empty.

He sat down and stretched his legs. It was peaceful here and he had not finished the process of sorting out his ideas. Where was Nita? Could it have been Nita who hit him? His mind was soon far away.

Near at hand, three newspapers slowly lowered. He found himself looking straight into the eyes of Uncle Hubert. Cousin Charlie was on one side and an elderly lady on the other. The two men were not smiling for the moment, but there was no mistaking those bland, cleft-chinned faces. The woman had small, fine features, in the Edwardian style, with rouge dabbed on like a doll and a broad choker necklace of big pearls.

"Have you seen Nita anywhere?"

His bombshell was carefully timed. Three newspapers fell, as though by drill, to three prosperous laps. There was a silence: a small pool of silence around only themselves, whilst outside the periphery there were waves of clapping and the straining of a cornet solo.

"So you are a friend of poor Nita's? I trust you have had no disturbing experiences?"

He looked at the older man as he spoke. His was a face which had not known the fret of worry or doubt for many years. Sitting down, he still looked a trifle top-heavy. His legs were abnormally short, and even an extremely expensive tailor had not been able to lengthen them.

"Disturbing experiences? Why should I?"

"That's good. Only wanted to be sure."

Cousin Charlie grinned back at him. There was nothing reassuring about his smile.

"I thought she seemed frightened about something. Don't you think we ought to try to find her?"

No one stopped to ask him how he knew of their existence or how he had recognized them. No one asked him his name.

Everything was cordial and trusting and cosy. Cosy, like a cobra. He found himself looking into dark brown eyes, wide open, unflickering and only slightly mascaraed. Aunt Marion was a fine looking woman.

"She shouldn't be out alone, really, poor child. I shouldn't say this to a stranger: but then, you know Nita well, don't you? When she ran away, naturally we didn't go to the police. But we must watch, mustn't we? Watch very carefully indeed?"

Her eyes had left his and were focused down, through a gap in the pier railing, towards a small jetty from which rowing boats were let out on hire. One boat had just recently pulled away and a man sitting in its stern was rowing with a slow, steady stroke.

"Whatever do you mean? Nita seems most normal to me."

Even as he said it, Phil found himself wondering how much he meant it, how sure he could be of its accuracy. Which in no way interrupted a tide of far stronger feeling for Nita.

"If you'd looked after her since she was a small girl, you'd understand. Poor child. One has to be most careful with her."

The three of them stood up. For no very good reason, Phil did the same.

Fifty yards away the boat was moving steadily. Suddenly his mind came back to earth; or, in this case, to sea.

The man who was rowing wore a bowler hat. He was fat, and from where they stood, the tops of long rubber boots were visible. Sitting, facing him, Nita, in her white dress, looked cool and beautiful and supremely composed. Beside her was Jimmy Westlake. He was talking. Phil could see his lips move, but the words did not reach across the intervening space.

Sharply, Uncle Hubert opened his mouth.

"Westlake! Hi! Westlake!"

The sound must have carried to Dieppe. Jimmy looked up, startled. But without a sign of recognition, he turned back to Nita and began to talk faster than ever. Methodically, the man in the bowler hat rowed on.

Beside Phil, Aunt Marion was watching: lips slightly apart, and eyes stretched wide. When he saw them, he knew that he would never be able to forget those wide brown eyes: kindly eyes, yet speculative and appraising like a hangman's on holiday.

At that moment he knew beyond doubt that he had stumbled into a world set at a strange angle: a dangerous world.

"Now, what?"

It was Phil who asked the question. He was not certain he wanted a reply.

V

ON UNCLE HUBERT'S TRAIL

Laurence Meynell

"NOW WHAT?" PHIL had asked uncertainly, and three bland, unhelpful faces were turned on him. Clearly there wasn't going to be much in the way of friendly co-operation from Uncle Hubert & Co.

The late afternoon was warm, sultry even, with thunder still lurking round, but Phil felt a sudden cold shiver. Definitely he didn't like the idea of Nita being in any way at their mercy.

He edged along the Pier a little and put in a spot of rapid thinking.

He realized that he was leaning up against a telescope, one of the fixed sideshows of the Pier, and to give himself some excuse for standing there he slipped a penny into the slot and having thus secured the instrument's release turned it idly on to the rowing boat with its improbable load.

It was farther away now and Sid was still pulling steadily, but not more steadily than Jimmy Westlake was talking. Jimmy was leaning towards Nita and talking fast and urgently. "In the name of God," Phil wondered, "what's he doing here and what's he talking about?"

But it was when he turned the telescope on to Nita, that Phil got his real shock. Cool and beautiful, he had thought she had looked, and supremely composed.

But with the telescope bringing that fantastic boat-load within touching distance, as it were, Phil changed his ideas. Cool and beautiful; yes, both these things still. But composed? If a set face drawn and white and fixed with fear is the same as composed, why then yes—composed.

"That kid's deadly scared," Phil thought and the expression "hypnotized with fear" bobbed up in his mind to alarm him.

He deserted the telescope; he reckoned he had had his pennyworth.

The three Gorgons had taken counsel and were sending an emissary. Uncle Hubert.

"Perhaps you would like to join us for a while," he suggested blandly, "and we could have a talk about how you came to know Nita?"

Will you walk into my parlour, Phil thought, and he felt the first beginnings of the excitement of the chase; for the moment he was a jump ahead of Uncle Hubert & Co., and he meant to keep there.

He glanced at his watch.

"'Fraid I haven't time. I only came down for the day. I must be getting back to the station."

Without a flicker Uncle Hubert said: "I'll walk up with you if I may. I want to find out details of the trains tomorrow."

"Don't bother—"

"No bother at all. I'd enjoy the walk—and your company."

Phil nodded agreement and the two of them set off.

". . . seeing me off the premises," Phil thought and the realization amused him more than anything else. There was always another card in the pack.

The streets of Breston were already beginning to show signs of preparation for the Carnival to be held that evening.

"Pity you're not staying for it," Uncle Hubert said sweetly.

Phil nodded. "Must get back," he mumbled.

When they reached the station they discovered that a fast train for London was due out in five minutes.

"Does it stop en route?" Uncle Hubert asked with interest.

"First stop Victoria, guv'nor."

Uncle Hubert seemed pleased.

At the head of Platform Five Phil suddenly discovered that he hadn't got, and must have, an evening paper.

"You stay here," Uncle Hubert told him. "I'll get you one."

It took him maybe a minute, no more, to cross to the bookstall and buy a *Star*. He thought he had his eye on Phil all 60 seconds of that minute. But he didn't: not quite. In the space in which Uncle Hubert said: "*Star*, please," handed his sixpence over and got his change, Phil had time to do something. He whisked a penny out of his pocket, rammed it into a platform ticket machine and secreted the ticket all with the speed of a conjurer. He had an idea that the penny ticket was going to come in handy shortly.

Uncle Hubert was back.

"Your paper," he said, "and there's three minutes to go."

"Well, thanks very much—"

"There is just one thing," the quiet bland voice went on, and it was as though the crack of a steel whip had suddenly been introduced into it.

The two men looked at one another.

"What's that?"

"Nita—I shouldn't worry about her if I were you. In fact, do you know, young man, I've an idea it will be quite a lot healthier for everybody if you just forget about Nita?"

The two men were still staring into each other's eyes and Phil only hoped he didn't look as scared as he suddenly felt.

"Okay," he said brightly. "Call it a day, eh? Suits me."

Uncle Hubert nodded. "I think that's very sensible of you," he said. "Very sensible indeed. Good-bye."

Phil went through the barrier and, half way up the platform, turned. Uncle Hubert was still standing there.

"Takes no chances," Phil thought. "Still, he hasn't seen everything—yet."

He waved, opened the door of a first smoker and went in. Time was getting short so he only waited for one whole minute and then he acted.

He crossed the carriage and, opening the door on the far side from the platform, slipped out. His own train, the fast to Victoria, was standing alongside a local one. Phil slipped on to the track and then scrambled up the side of the local train, painfully barking a shin in the process. He managed to gain access to a carriage (which luckily was empty) and went straight through it on to the platform beyond.

Just as he gained the platform he heard the whistle blowing which meant that the express was pulling out.

Phil grinned to himself, highly satisfied. "Nice work," he thought.

At the head of the platform he gave up his platform ticket and, with great caution, emerged into the maelstrom of people in the general station.

Uncle Hubert had just turned and was walking away; walking away with a smile on his unpleasant face. The interfering young fool, whose interest in Nita might have been very awkward, was safely on his way to London, Uncle Hubert thought, unaware that at that precise moment the interfering young fool, limping slightly because of a painful scraped shin, was barely thirty yards behind, following him through the crowd.

VI

TROUBLE AT THE YELLOW CAT

Laurence Meynell

"WHERE NOW?" PHIL wondered happily. He reckoned that so far he was getting very good value for his penny platform ticket.

He had taken a strong dislike to Uncle Hubert and his fellow waxworks, and he was possessed of an overwhelming curiosity to know what was happening to Nita; and when he thought again of that beautiful face set rigid with fear as she sat in that preposterous little boat, his dislike of the man he was following grew considerably.

The streets were beginning to fill with people awaiting the Carnival procession, and it was a simple matter to keep in touch without being noticed.

At first they headed for the Front and Phil thought, "must be back to the Pier", then his quarry turned suddenly into a small opening and plunged into a mass of side streets and alleyways. Here the shadowing game was far less easy, but there were plenty of corners and Phil managed to keep out of sight.

At the end of a narrow alley which boasted a couple of unprosperous-looking junk shops and a dubious photographer's, Uncle Hubert disappeared smartly into what, when Phil cautiously came up to it, turned out to be The Yellow Cat Café.

For ten minutes Phil hung about uncertainly, and then, not knowing whether he was acting wisely or not, he plucked up courage and went in.

The Yellow Cat was singularly unprepossessing inside and trade appeared to be slack. At a table in the centre sat three men all of whom Phil disliked on sight, particularly the bald one with heavy lidded eyes and cauliflower ears. If ever three people had "thug" written well and truly on their ugly faces, those three have, he thought.

Of Uncle Hubert there was not a sign. A staircase led up to—what?

When he had given his order to the horse-faced woman who came to take it, he put the query to her.

"That's private up there," she told him and she shot a look at him which was hard to decipher exactly—apprehensive, curious, warning?

She disappeared into the kitchen parts to get his roes on toast and Phil immediately acted. Keeping a wary eye on the committee meeting of thugs at the centre table, he made his way to the stairs and began to go up. The odd thing was that not one of the three took any notice; they were aware of what he was doing, of that he was sure, but they didn't take any notice; and somehow that studied lack of interest struck Phil as being highly sinister.

At the top was a curtain; he pushed through it, glad to be beyond it and out of sight.

It smelt musty and dirty; on the other side was a

door marked "Private" so naturally Phil tried the handle, found that it turned and let himself through.

He found himself on a dark stone landing from the far side of which a flight of equally dark stone stairs led down somewhere. Phil crossed and had a look down, and could see little except darkness and a dustbin vaguely glimpsed at the bottom. Presumably it gave on to a yard: must be useful he thought as a second line of approach for whoever used the top parts of The Yellow Cat.

He stood on the landing for a moment or two to consider, and began to repent his impetuosity in coming up there.

Roes on toast didn't take all that time to prepare and the horse-faced one would soon be returning with them. Presumably she would then inquire from the thug trio what had happened to her customer and the fat would be in the fire. At which moment two distinct and unpleasant sounds assailed Phil's ears, one after the other.

The first was a moan. There could be no doubting that that was what he heard: a low moan of pain and despair mixed.

Whether it came from man or woman he didn't know; but he knew where the sound that followed it came from. It was a high-pitched laugh and if a sound ever deserved to be called fiendish that one did. It came from Uncle Hubert, and hardly had the spittle begun to flow in Phil's dried throat again when a door at the end of the small landing opened and Uncle Hubert himself came out.

Phil pressed back into the dark shadows and stood stock still, scarcely breathing.

Uncle Hubert came to the top of the stairs and

peered down. Was he expecting anyone, Phil wondered, or just reassuring himself that no one was there?

At that moment not four feet separated the men, and though Phil had by this time ceased to breathe, something made the other turn. Slowly he turned his bland turtle face and they were looking at each other. Except that he was scared stiff, Phil could have laughed at the other's surprise.

"God in Heaven," Uncle Hubert whispered, *"the young interfering fool again! Why couldn't you keep out of it, my friend?"*

The whisper and the silence into which it faded were broken by the sudden noisy grating of a door below. Somebody had entered the back way and was even now beginning to come up the dark stairs.

Phil thought more rapidly than he had ever done before in his life; he thought, "I'm getting out of here quick and if this is a pal of the gang's coming up, so much the worse for him." Without a second's hesitation he flung himself past Uncle Hubert's outstretched arm down the dark stairway.

He hit whoever it was coming up on about the fourth step and they rolled together to the bottom, all the breath knocked out of both of them.

Phil was the first up. He could see the back door of the place ajar and he meant to be outside.

And when he took a look at the man he had brought crashing to the stone floor with a frightful clatter of the waiting dustbin he wanted to get outside more than ever.

A policeman was lying there. And he was lying in a very awkward-looking way. Certainly he was unconscious, and he might be dead.

Phil didn't stop to find out.

"*God Almighty*," he said to himself, "*that's torn it.*" And pushing his way out through the half open back door he did a very foolish thing—he started to run.

VII

ACCIDENT AT THE MILL

Joan Fleming

As PHILIP COURTNEY ran he felt with his hand the lump at the back of his head. It was very swollen and quite numb, and the back of his neck felt extremely stiff and sore. He wondered if he were seeing double, decided it was not so; but his brain felt as though it was hung with cobwebs. He felt as though he were running around in a nightmare, unaccountably heavy-footed; everything, he thought, was all right really, soon he would wake up in bed at the Royal Scarlet Hotel with a bad attack of indigestion.

But first he had to get back to the Fun Fair, where it had all started.

The Fair Ground had been crowded when, years and years ago (in fact, some few hours previously), he had stood in front of Ye Olde Haunted Mill, staring at the bowler-hatted barker and idly jingling the loose change in his pocket. Now the crowd had coagulated in front of that particular attraction, and it was such that Phil realized at once that something was wrong.

"What's up?" he asked a man on the outskirts of the throng.

"Been a nasty accident," was the answer and, looking more closely at his informant, Phil recognized him as the man who always stands on the edge of crowds, on tiptoe, neck stretched, a gleam of excitement in his eye, hoping for the worst. Clearly the man knew nothing, but clearly, also, something had happened. There was an ambulance standing on the asphalt fairway, there were two police cars and a number of police officials of various ranks.

Phil tried to elbow his way through the crowd, but they resisted him with some hostility; why should this big young man get any better view than they themselves? They stood their ground. He remembered his old regimental badge which, for no particular reason, he kept pinned at the back of his left lapel. He flipped his lapel now with a professional flick: "CID!" he hissed out of the corner of his mouth and the crowd fell away before him even as the Red Sea opened in front of Moses and the Israelites.

Standing with her back to the crowd, watching the openings of the two tunnels at the entrance to the cavern, stood the blonde with the bikini bathing suit, the one who had led the laughter at his expense as he had emerged, wading from the tunnel. Phil, about to fling his leg over the barrier and enter the small forecourt, hesitated. She would recognize him, of course . . .

Then, with a sense of shame, he remembered the

beautiful grey eyes, wide with terror, of Nita Ross.
"Some Knight Errant!" he thought scornfully and,
throwing caution to the winds, he vaulted lightly
over the barrier.

The bikini girl turned at once. Though a chilly
east wind had sprung up she remained as warm-
looking, as smoothly sunburned as before, but he
now realized that she was a tough baby of some
thirty-nine summers.

"They're bringing out the body," someone in the
crowd behind him said.

"What body?" someone else asked. "I reckon
it's a stunt to popularize Ye Olde Haunted Mill. The
place is full of bodies, horrible wax images done up
to terrify."

For a full moment Phil stared at the blonde baby
in the bikini and she stared back at him without the
slightest recognition lighting her features.

"Who are they bringing out?" he asked.

"A young girl. Foul play. They think she's been
murdered," the blonde answered, rolling the words
around with some relish. "They don't like real bodies around this joint, so the dicks have got a hustle
on to get her away." She went on, with a burst of
information: "They've been taking photographs in
there. See those johnnies," she nudged Phil.

A macabre procession appeared at the mouth of
one of the tunnels; stretcher-bearers, wading in the
stream, their trousers rolled up, their legs and feet a
livid white. The barefooted ambulance men shuffled
towards the ambulance with their burden, a small,
still figure, covered with a shroud.

It was suddenly absolutely necessary to Phil that
he should know whose body lay upon the stretcher.

It was unthinkable that it could be that of Nita Ross, that lovely, lively girl in the white frock. And yet it was equally impossible that it could not be, for had she not dug her fingernails into his wrist in very real terror of—something?

The blonde baby was not looking at the gruesome procession, she was watching Phil. Poised upon the balls of his feet he was clearly going to swoop forward as the stretcher passed him and fling back that shroud.

But the bikini baby was every bit as quick a thinker as Phil Courtney. Seizing his arm, she drew him towards her. Phil tried to shake her off, but she held him in a vice-like grip.

"Who is it? I must know who it is!"

"Here . . ." she drew him aside, behind the pay desk.

"Do you know who it is?"

"Sure . . . I'll tell you . . . but first . . . honey chile . . ."

Phil found himself being kissed. As everyone knows, there are kisses and kisses, and this was one of those: it lasted for the duration, that is, until the stretcher and the corpse were packed away, the doors of the ambulance snapped shut, the driver smartly in his seat and the equipage ringing its way through the crowd and away.

They both came out of the kiss breathless; the blonde started to tidy her hair. Phil took her by the shoulders and shook her.

"Tell me who it is. You said you'd tell."

"A young girl, dearie."

Phil moaned. "But who? What was her name?"

"How should I know?"

"Where's the owner of this show? Sid . . . he was fixing the jets?"

"Sid's 'opped it. Can't afford to get mixed up with the dicks, can't Sid."

It was, then, undoubtedly, Sid who had been rowing out in the bay. And that being so, there was not much doubt that his passengers, as Phil had observed, were Nita and his friend and publisher, Jimmy Westlake.

Who, then, was the "young girl" whose body had been so hastily removed from Ye Olde Haunted Mill?

Phil's pulses settled down as he realized that, after all, Nita was still alive. The one thing he must do now was to find her, even if it meant hiring a speed boat and following the rowing boat out into the bay. With this object in view he prepared to vault the barrier and to remove himself from the scene.

But the blonde baby clutched his arm. "Not so fast, ducky!" She had an extraordinary grip; Phil wondered if, as a side-line, she was a champion weight-lifter.

"Look," he said, "you may be a very fine professional kisser, but that's as far as it goes, see? You'll get out of my way now or I'll be obliged to get rough!"

"Officer, officer!" the blonde baby shrieked. "Here's the man I saw wading out of the tunnel shortly after the current was stopped!"

Two plain-clothes men walked across from the mouth of the cavern.

"And look!" she went on, "look what I've found in his pocket!"

From Phil's pocket she drew two photographs. Photographs of smiling men with cleft chins, the photographs which Phil had seen Nita hand to Sid, the owner of the Haunted Mill. Phil had given the unwilling Sid one pound sterling to keep those photographs beside him at the pay desk so that he might watch for two similar, smiling faces.

But the thing that staggered Phil was not so much the reappearance of the photographs from his own pocket, nor the sleight-of-hand trick which had got them there; it was the question as to where abouts on her person, which was covered with mere inches of material, the blonde had concealed the photographs.

"Here's the man I was telling you about, officer," the blonde baby said helpfully, with a bright smile.

VIII

AN INSPECTOR CALLS . . .

Joan Fleming

"WE LIVE," INSPECTOR A. said smoothly, "in a fantastic world, at present. Murders, assassinations, abductions, secret weapons—what have you.

"But then we live in the atom age and after the explosion of the atom bomb why—anything is possible.

"Here you have a set-up apparently quite normal: a young girl, Nita Ross, living in a respectable district of London with her Uncle Hubert, her Cousin Charles and her Aunt Marion. Terror that her loving relations are suddenly determined to kill her seizes the girl.

"She runs away from home, fleeing to Breston with the idea that she will be unnoticed by any pursuers amongst the vast polyglot holiday crowds in this particular town. In a moment of hysterical panic, recognizing you by sight, she asks you for protection. That is her story. So far so good."

They were sitting in Philip Courtney's bedroom at

The Royal Scarlet Hotel: Inspector A., Sergeant B. and Phil Courtney himself, now pale and distracted-looking.

The meeting being an informal one, there was a bottle of Scotch between them on the table. Phil had taken a couple of aspirins to assuage the raging pain in his head; he felt better now, though his head was far from clear.

There was something, caught up there in the cobwebs which hung about his brain, that he wanted to remember. Something that he knew he should remember, *must* remember . . . what was it?

"And now *our* story," Inspector A. went on after a long pull at his tumbler. "These three precious relations, uncle, cousin and aunt, call up their local police and ask for protection. Their house is being watched, they say. Their niece was followed as she left the house upon three occasions—so they say. They suspect that a full-scale burglary is being planned.

"Next, the whole family leave their home in charge of their local police, and go to Breston, the girl by a morning train and her relations by a train later in the day. The girl puts up at this hotel and the relations at another. What next? An urgent phone call from the Fun Fair—female in charge of Ye Olde Haunted Mill has found a real corpse lying around among the fake ones. That of a young girl."

The inspector again applied himself to his tumbler. "And now *your* story . . . and lastly . . . photographs of Uncle Hubert and Cousin Charles produced from your jacket pocket."

"By a trick," Phil put in.

The inspector bowed his head slightly in recognition of the remark. "By, as you declare, a clever trick. Would it interest you to know that Cousin Charles and Uncle Hubert spent quite a lot of time in the Isle of Man some years ago? Incarcerated—for security reasons. Would it also interest you to know that Aunt Marion spent nine months in Holloway Jail some eleven years ago for activities aimed at impeding our war effort?"

Phil leaned forward: "What does interest me," he said, "is the fact that the girl Nita Ross is aged somewhere between nineteen and twenty-two. Couldn't be more. She has only lived with her grim relations since she was ten."

Inspector A. drained his glass and leaned back in his chair. "We have reason to believe," he said, "that the Three Wicked Relations, as we may call them, are the pawns of a superior mind. You'll nearly always find," he threw off lightly, "that the master-mind in this sort of set-up chooses, as a rule, to keep himself well out of the ordinary rough-and-tumble. He never strikes in person unless he's pretty sure he's not going to get found out. He leaves the bad shots, the hit-or-miss methods, to others. When *he* strikes—that's *it*."

Phil shuddered, remembering the hideous aftermath of that striking and the shuffling stretcher-bearers.

"A dead girl," continued the inspector, "of somewhere between nineteen and twenty-two, with fair hair, was found lying in Ye Olde Haunted Mill, arranged carefully, beneath some dirty sacking and straw, beside the old water wheel. The original wax corpse had been stuffed out of sight behind some of that ghastly scenery. The intention had clearly been that the girl should remain there until— er—natural processes caused the murder to be discovered; by which time the murderer could cover his tracks pretty adequately. A clever idea!"

Phil cleared his throat. "What was she wearing?"

"Navy blue slacks and a white suntop. She had been stabbed."

"It was the wrong girl," Phil croaked. "They murdered the wrong girl! Nita was wearing a white frock. She may have been seen at some time or other, perhaps even this morning, wearing the clothes you describe. They are ordinary enough, walking the length of the promenade you might meet half a dozen girls wearing navy slacks and a white suntop." He paused. "If you can find those items of clothing amongst Nita's luggage that'll prove they made a mistake."

"It is possible," Inspector A. pronounced, "but it's not like our master-mind to make a silly mistake."

"But it would be easy," Phil urged. "You said yourself that the master-mind didn't do the dirty work, he always gets someone else to do it for him. He tells his hired assassin to follow a girl in navy blue slacks and a white suntop, and there you are.

"This morning she was probably wearing the slacks and suntop: in the afternoon she changed her clothes, putting on the white silk frock. It's just the sort of thing the master-mind might fall down on; a woman's whim, the desire to change her clothes."

"Hum." It was not Inspector A.'s habit to have theories expounded to him; he liked to be the theorizer. Nevertheless, he could not fail to be impressed by this young man's prescience.

"Well, Mr—er—Courtney," he said. "Since you seem to have a bit of a master-mind yourself, you'd better find your Miss Nita Ross for me, and PDQ. I'd like a talk with her."

"Look," Phil said, really the Knight Errant at last, "you keep your eye on the ball, Inspector." As they had made big strides in their acquaintanceship in the last hour, this remark did not sound disagreeable. "That elderly blonde down at Ye Olde Haunted Mill . . ."

"You mean the one with the—er—," Inspector A. described certain wavy lines about his own body.

"The same," Phil said curtly.

"We know all about her," Inspector A. said triumphantly.

"I think, now," Phil said with a smile which he hoped was full of sinister innuendoes, "this very minute she's preparing to do a bolt, is my guess. If possible with her boy-friend, Sid, of the bowler hat and the waders . . ."

When, at last, he had shaken off Inspector A. and his satellite with the remark that whatever happened next he, personally, must have a sleep, Phil snatched up his binoculars and looked out to sea.

The bay was swept clean of small pleasure craft, the water rippled with the stiffish breeze. A mile or so out in the bay a small yacht had been anchored all day, exciting comment and some admiration from the holiday crowds. This elegant little craft was now no more than recognizable as such through Phil's binoculars. It was steaming away towards the horizon.

It wasn't a ten-to-one chance that the girl with the grey eyes was on board. It was a cert.

IX

THE WOMAN IN ROOM 220

Michael Cronin

RESTING HIS ELBOWS on the window-sill, he gave himself another and a larger look: and mentally and so devoutly he was wishing himself across the intervening space of rippling sun-lit water.

As he watched, the yacht seemed to change shape and he saw that it was altering course, presenting him now with a broadside view: smart and very modern lines, probably twin Diesels with a nice solid turn of speed; within a small compass, comparatively luxurious; a rich man's hobby exclusively.

And Nita Ross with the bright hair and the fear in her grey eyes? Was he fooling himself? Where *was* she? And Jimmy Westlake and that small rowing boat?

He blinked. But there was nothing wrong with his vision: the yacht had stopped; straining his eyes he caught the leaping prow of a speedboat circling round the larger craft, throwing white foam as it cut through and across the waves.

The speedboat swerved close in under the yacht's
stern and then swung out and away; the yacht was
moving again, and considerably faster than before,
heading straight out to sea; the speedboat was forced
to make a much wider circuit and, now well clear of
the shore calm, it was hitting the swell viciously.

Phil Courtney watched this crazy performance. It
reminded him of a fighter beating up a transport
plane: presently the speedboat skidded off and went
roaring across the bay, leaving a wide curving sweep
of foam . . . and the motor-yacht went steadily on its
way at a respectable rate of knots.

He removed himself from his perch and thoughtfully gave himself a further dose of what was left of
the Scotch on the table by his bed. Some chaotic
ideas were churning around in his head. He checked
his wallet: ammunition was a first essential, the
universal folding stuff.

The lift was full: the cocktail hour was on, and the
Royal Scarlet Hotel at the height of the season makes
quite a thing of its assortment of American Bars,
Tudor Lounges, Cocktail Parlours, and what-have-you.

He pushed his way through the throng on the
ground floor: one or two smart pieces perched on
stools at strategic points gave him a "how-about-it"
but he didn't even see them.

The manager was in his office. He was a very
smooth character: celebrities were very much his cup
of tea. And in his own sphere, Philip Courtney was
undeniably a celebrity: COURTNEY FOR CRIME jumped
at you from hoardings, newspaper columns, cinema
screens.

Cash a cheque for Mr Courtney? But of course—

how much? Not at all, Mr Courtney, not at all a pleasure . . . fifty?

The money made a pleasant bulge in his pocket.

"Did Miss Ross leave an envelope for me?" he said.

"Miss Ross? No, Mr Courtney."

"Damn," said Phil. "That's going to hold me up. She's been doing some research for me and has some notes I need . . . and I know she'll be out all the evening."

The manager was politely sympathetic.

"Urgent work, I suppose?"

"Very. Publisher waiting for it."

"Could I have a chambermaid look in her room?"

"No," said Phil, "she wouldn't know what to look for. I expect Nita brought a pile of papers with her . . . associate editor of Westlake's you know: very busy girl. I've got it—just let me have her key and I'll pop up and look myself. . . and I'll leave her a rude note into the bargain. How's that?"

"Well, it's strictly against our regulations, Mr Courtney . . . you appreciate that?"

"Not a word from me," said Phil, "and you'll be doing me a real favour."

He got the key. Room 220. Second floor front, the opposite wing to his own. He was going to allow himself five or ten minutes for this, no more. Whatever he did next, it seemed to him to be a wise precaution to have a very quick look at her room before he started rushing off in all directions. *Her* room. How little he really knew of her . . . and yet how much she mattered already, *really* mattered to him.

So this was to be a quick pilgrimage—with a

vague hope of finding something, some pointer that might begin to lead him . . . girls wrote and received letters and kept diaries—at least in Courtney stories they invariably did when the plot required.

He bounced along the corridor, the key had a large brass tag: No. 220. And it rattled noisily as he thrust the key in the lock and turned it energetically.

She had done herself well: there was a tiny hall, a vestibule with a cream rug and two doors. It might have been his imagination, but the place seemed still to hold the fragrance of her personality.

The door in front of him was ajar and he pushed it open. The bright evening sun flooded the small neat room and for a moment he stood in the doorway, blinded by the radiance off the water. There was a stir in a corner to his left and a calm elderly female voice said:

"Come in and shut the door."

She was standing by a small brocaded armchair and a shaft of brilliant sunshine cut her in two at the waist, leaving her top half shadowed. But he knew it was Aunt Marion even before she moved towards him. The thick choker necklace of pearls gleamed against her thin neck, and the doll-like dabs of colour on her cheeks were a cosmetic caricature. But most important of all: she had a gun, and there was nothing grandmotherly in the way she was handling it.

"You learn nothing," she said thinly. "You are a fool and a nuisance." Her brown eyes assessed him without pleasure—and dismissed him. He had a strange unreal sensation . . . middle-aged women didn't do this sort of thing.

"Now look here—" he began.

"Drop that key, drop it on the floor; no, don't throw it."

"You're quite crazy," he said.

"The key," she repeated.

The brass tag chinked as he dropped it on to the carpet.

"Now go in there."

He hesitated. A Courtney hero would have a very neat way of coping with a situation such as this.

Carefully he walked in through the door she indicated; and Aunt Maron kept a very safe distance from him. Nita's bedroom—and what a way to enter it, at the point of a gun.

"Now, your shoes and trousers."

"No." He turned around and faced her. "This is just a little too fantastic—be your age, old dear."

"Take them off."

He sat on the edge of Nita's bed and he felt nothing like as debonair as he hoped he looked.

"No," he said. "Come and get them, Auntie."

Without fuss she fired from the waist. The gun went *phut* and the glass on the dressing table splintered. A very special and effective silencer.

"The next is for you," she said blandly, "in the stomach." So there he was, all by himself, locked in Nita Ross's bedroom, minus shoes and trousers, a most unheroic Knight Errant.

X

THE NOTE IN THE BOTTLE

Michael Cronin

AUNT MARION HAD evidently been conducting a very hurried search: the bedroom was chaotic: Nita Ross's wardrobe was extensive and most of it was spread about the floor.

He found some smartly-tailored navy slacks but they weren't of the slightest use to him. He tried himself against the bedroom door and lost decisively.

Down below in the sunshine were the rows of cars and the lawns and the bright orange umbrellas for the outside drinkers. Directly beneath him by the wall sat a solitary character in a blazer with a pint tankard in front of him.

Phil found an elegant shoe and wrote a brief note: "Please send manager Room 220. Am locked in. Have one on me." He stuffed the message and a ten shilling note into the toe of the shoe, wrapped a nylon stocking around it, and heaved it out of the window.

* * *

The reaction of the pint drinker was immediate: perhaps the nylon did it. He looked up with open-mouthed interest, hoping, no doubt, for a poppet in distress. Phil waved at him. The other read the message again, finished his beer, gave Phil a thumbs-up, and went inside; he hid his disappointment like a gentleman.

At first the manager took a poor view of the situation; even for a fashionable crime-writer this was, he felt, a bit too much. Then Phil Courtney did some very fast talking: the whole thing was a joke, just a joke—some film boys had seen him entering Miss Ross's apartment . . . they'd knocked on the door, and when he let them in they'd debagged him and cleared off.

"I see," said the manager. "I doubt if Miss Ross would approve."

"I'm sure she wouldn't . . . be a good chap and bring me some trousers and shoes."

The manager paused at the door. "There are no film people staying here, Mr Courtney, that I can remember."

"Visitors," said Phil glibly. "Saw me downstairs and followed me . . . I apologize for them . . . no harm done. All I want is some clothes, please."

Ten minutes later he was going down the front steps of the Royal Scarlet. The boy by the wall was back in position; instead of a pint there was a large whisky. As Phil passed he gave him a large wink.

"Pretty thin story, old boy—who was it—her boy friend?"

Phil grinned at him. "You're smart," he said. "You know this place?"

"I live here, old son. Why?"

"I want to hire a fast motor-launch, maybe for a longish trip. Really fast, I mean. Could be an all-night job."

Some of the whisky was lowered. "Legitimate?"

"Naturally. No strings. I'll pay twenty-five and the petrol."

The rest of the whisky went very rapidly. The other man got to his feet.

"The name's Joe," he said. "Joe Fawcett. Know everyone in the place."

Phil introduced himself and was relieved to find that the name Courtney meant nothing to Joe Fawcett.

"Got just the bloke for you," said Joe. "Peter Tooley—if he's in. Hop in and hold on."

The car was a very pre-war sports model; bright red, no springing and plenty of noise. They bundled along the Front and the evening crowds were thicker than ever.

At Phil's request they turned in towards the Fun Fair at the west end. Ye Olde Haunted Mill was doing no business at all; the tunnels of mystery were boarded up.

Joe knew the pair who ran the outfit; Sid and Thelma.

"Pair of twisters, chum—leave 'em alone, strictly. Thelma's a so-and-so . . . take it from me. Looks like they've scarpered."

"I wouldn't be surprised," said Phil. "Let's press on."

He was watching the expanse of bright sea as they came to the end of the promenade; there was a collier ploughing her way up from the south-west and a top-heavy pleasure steamer nosing in to the pier from the island; no smart motor-yacht—she would be well clear of the headland by now . . . visibility seemed to be closing in.

They found Peter Tooley in a wooden shed at the end of a short stone jetty inside the old harbour; he had a large ginger moustache, a faded blue shirt and a lot of muscle.

Was he *interested*? For 25 smackers and expenses he'd charter the *Queen Mary*. And not too many questions asked.

"I want to catch up with a motor-yacht that pulled out of the bay about thirty minutes back," said Phil.

"The *Santa Monica*. Came in this morning—nice job. I've never seen her in here before. Friends of yours?" Peter Tooley was lifting oilskins from pegs.

"Kind of," said Phil. "Think you could make it?"

"If the weather lets us. There's a mist coming in off the sea. Might come unstuck . . . we'll have a stab."

It was a 40-foot sea-going launch, with a small cabin for'ard, not much comfort, but loads of urge: named inappropriately *Prudence*. Joe Fawcett waved them off from the jetty; he would have liked to join the party, but nobody invited him.

Phil sat in a crackling oilskin in the small well behind the cabin door; the engine rumbled powerfully and the slender hull trembled; once they cleared the green calm inside the jetty they started to roll and he was reminded very forcibly of the bump on the back of his head—and the fact that he had missed a meal or two.

Peter Tooley stood by the wheel with an unlit pipe upside down in his mouth; according to him the *Santa Monica* must have been on a south-westerly course—unless the skipper was proposing to run across the Channel at night, and with that mist coming up Peter thought that unlikely.

As soon as they cleared the headland they really met the mist: it was like running into a faint enshrouding curtain that parted in front of them and closed in again behind. *Prudence* slackened speed; it was no longer an inviting summer sea; it was grey and forbidding.

Peter Tooley's moustache was limp and he used some nautical language.

"Might clear if we find a bit of wind . . . you want to go on?"

Phil nodded. He was smoking a cigarette and not enjoying it: all of a sudden the bright idea didn't seem so bright after all: this was a job for Inspector A. with all his resources but then Inspector A. didn't really believe him, or did he?

They found a clear patch, increased speed for a few hundred yards, and then ran into another drifting blanket of mist that brought them almost to a full stop. *Prudence* rolled unpleasantly.

"Hey," said Peter Tooley, "I've just remembered something . . . might interest you if you've got friends on the *Santa Monica*: Bert Roper was telling me about it just before you showed up.

"He runs a speedboat and this afternoon he was giving some girl a special thrill out in the bay . . . so he 'buzzes' the *Santa Monica,* gave her the real treatment: according to Bert he pretty nearly took the paint off her once or twice. They didn't like it on the *Santa Monica*—Bert says there was a fight and somebody heaved a bottle at him—it pretty nearly took his head off.

"There was a kind of note inside for somebody named Courtney at the Royal Scarlet. It was signed with the initials 'JW'. *Courtney*—cripes, is that you?"

"It is—what did the note say?"

"Something about Tollard Point at dawn tomorrow . . . Bert's taken it up to the Royal Scarlet, looking for you—that's a laugh, isn't it?"

"Is it?" said Phil grimly. "We're going back. Reverse, brother, or whatever you do to these things."

Dawn tomorrow: Tollard Point: the *Santa Monica* . . . "JW" was Jimmy Westlake: and what about Inspector A.'s Master Mind of crime? And Nita? Especially Nita Ross.

XI

PHIL LASHES OUT

Elizabeth Ferrars

As PHIL COURTNEY walked up the beach towards the Royal Scarlet, two thoughts were contending for dominance in his mind. One was simply the thought of food. Good food, bad food, any food, so long as it was lots of food. Almost nostalgically, his mind went back to the roes on toast that he ordered but had not remained to eat in The Yellow Cat. A regrettable mistake, he felt. Boy scouts and knights errant should keep their strength up.

The second thought was of Jimmy Westlake.

Jimmy Westlake, his publisher, a quiet, baldish, rather anxious man, always fretting about something, the shortage of paper, the costs of production, the international situation.

Jimmy Westlake, who had made that preposterous bet with Phil, so out of keeping, really, with all that Phil knew of his character.

Jimmy Westlake, who had been determined to get Phil Courtney to Breston.

That last was obvious. Whatever it was that had brought Jimmy Westlake himself to Breston, at the same time as Nita Ross and Nita Ross's unattractive relatives, it had not been by chance that he had persuaded, argued, almost pestered Phil into going there, too.

At the reception-desk in the hotel Phil asked: "Any messages for me?"

The clerk glanced at his pigeon-hole and shook his head.

"But there was a man here called Roper inquiring for you, Mr Courtney," he said. "He said he'd come back."

"I see, thanks."

Phil walked towards the bar. A quick drink, he thought, and then dinner, for until his hunger was assuaged he would be quite unable to think clearly. As things were, his imagination had become so troublesomely occupied with morbidly seductive visions of roes on toast that he was not even able to make up his mind whether he believed that that message in the bottle had been the desperate attempt by a man in mortal danger to get help, or a trap.

But did it matter which it was? Phil had no doubt at all that he was going to keep the dawn appointment at Tollard Point.

He took his first sip of a Martini and at that precise moment a very extraordinary thing happened.

It started with a curious sensation as if something in him were about to explode. But that was only the beginning of it. Next, all the crazy events of the afternoon, each making an isolated picture, painted in lurid colours, began to spin round and round in his brain. Then all at once they settled. That was the extraordinary part of the experience. They settled in a pattern and, to Phil's astonished mind, made sense.

"Roes on toast!" he said aloud.

The white-jacketed waiter moved towards him.

"Yes, sir?" he said helpfully.

"The Yellow Cat!" Phil exclaimed, not even aware that the waiter had spoken.

"No, sir, I shouldn't, if I were you," the man said. "It's not a good class sort of place—you wouldn't like it."

Phil pulled himself together. But though he managed to keep his next thoughts to himself, his eyes continued to dwell with such baleful intensity on the waiter's face that the man grew uneasy and after an instant edged away.

The fact was that until that moment Phil had been trying not to think of The Yellow Cat. He had no idea what the penalties were for assaulting a policeman, but he thought vaguely that they were immeasurably heavy. Years and years in jail, perhaps. And he had not liked the way that that policeman had stayed huddled at the foot of the stairs.

It was because of these feelings that Phil had failed to ask himself a simple question.

Who had moaned?

Who was it who, as Phil came creeping along the squalid landing, had given the moan of fear and despair that he had overheard and that had been followed so hideously by Uncle Hubert's sadistic laughter?

Now Phil not only asked himself this question, but in doing so he knew the answer. He stood up. The waiter looked relieved to see him go, but watched him with a certain wariness until he had disappeared through the revolving doors.

A minute or two later, however, Phil was back and the waiter reluctantly took his order for another Martini. While he was mixing it Phil opened the evening paper that he had just bought and looked through it hurriedly.

The item in which he was interested had been front-page news a week before. Now Phil found only a few lines on page three. He read:

"Information was received in London yesterday that Dr Martin Gavenitz, the nuclear physicist who disappeared from his home in Surbiton last Wednesday, had been seen in a café in the town of Karlsruhe in Western Germany. It has now been reported, however, that the man seen in the café was a Mr John MacGregor, of Glasgow, on holiday in Germany with his wife and three children. The hunt for the missing scientist continues.

"One result of his disappearance, according to Mr James Westlake, publisher of Dr Gavenitz's recent book, *Atomic Power and Human Society,* is that this book has now passed into the best-seller class.

" 'I do not believe that Dr Gavenitz has been kidnapped or that he has fled behind the Iron Curtain,' Mr Westlake said. 'He is probably taking a quiet holiday somewhere and does not even know that he has been missed. He is a great man for whom I have the highest regard.' "

A quiet holiday, yes, Phil thought, in The Yellow Cat at Breston, while the *Santa Monica* waited in the bay to take him—where?

Wherever the pay was highest nowadays for kidnapped men of genius.

But where did Nita come in? And why had Jimmy Westlake, after treacherously delivering the scientist into the custody of the unspeakable Uncle Hubert, arranged that Phil Courtney should go to Breston?

"Mr Courtney?"

Phil lowered the paper to see who had spoken to him.

A big man in a loose raincoat stood there. He had a square, heavy, ruddy face and great shoulders. For some reason, Phil felt that he had seen him before.

"Are you Bert Roper?" he asked.

"No. I am a police officer," the man answered, "and I must ask you to accompany me."

Something cold slid down Phil's spine. Though the man was in plain clothes, there was no doubt about it, he was the policeman whom Phil had last seen lying in an ugly heap at the foot of the staircase in The Yellow Cat.

Phil gulped the rest of his drink.

"Am I under arrest?" he asked.

"No, sir," the man said, "but Inspector A. would like to see you.

Phil nodded and stood up. He thought of Tollard Point, of the dawn, of Jimmy Westlake and of Nita.

Then, for a second time, with all his strength, he drove his fist into the man's face and ran for it.

XII

A WRAITH COMES OUT
OF THE SEA

Elizabeth Ferrars

THE FOG SAVED Phil, the fog and a revolving door
which filled, a moment after Phil had shot through
it, with a number of chattering, undecided people,
who first thought they wanted to go into the Royal
Scarlet, then thought they didn't. By the time that
the policeman and all the well-intentioned people
who wanted to help him had managed to thrust their
way out of the hotel, Phil was fifty yards away,
invisible in the damp, clinging mist that was rolling
in from the sea.

He remembered not to run. He walked quietly the
length of the promenade, then straight on through
some gardens, along a few suburban streets and at
last out on to the cliff road. After the first moments
he had heard no sounds of pursuit.

Tollard Point, he knew, was about five miles away.
The cliffs were high there, with a narrow flight of
steps cut down the side of them to a small and

beautiful cove at the foot. The thought of feeling his way down those slippery and uneven steps in a fog made Phil feel slightly sick, yet he also thought with dread that the fog might lift before he got there.

On the way he stopped at a tobacconist's for some cigarettes and a bar of chocolate. He munched the chocolate as he walked. The fog was as thick as ever when he found the steps and started down them.

It seemed to take him an hour to reach the bottom, and by the time that he felt the shingle crunch under his feet his forehead was sticky with sweat as well as with the sea-mist. Standing still there, he waited and listened, but heard only the soft whispering of the calm water.

He heard nothing else for hours. Shivering, exhausted, utterly depressed and more than half-convinced that his mind had given way and that for the last twelve hours he had been suffering from delusions, he crouched on a rock or walked about, swinging his arms and talking to himself. At last, for a short time, he actually fell asleep.

The sound of a shot woke him.

Jerking as convulsively as if he had been shot himself, Phil stumbled to his feet, not knowing whether the shot had been dream or reality. Then other shots followed, then faint shouts, a splash and more shots. The sounds seemed to be quite close at hand, yet they all came from the sea.

Edging quietly up to the water's edge, Phil peered into the fog. It had changed while he slept. Not only had it become a little less dense, but there was a pale greyness in it, a first faint hint of the dawn. But though he knew the *Santa Monica* must be out there, he could still see nothing.

Then he saw something moving in the water.

Looking round him for some kind of weapon, he could only see stones. Stooping, he chose one, tried the feel of it, then waited, poised.

Out of the water came Nita.

At first, when she saw him standing there, a shadowy figure waiting for her, panic overcame her and she seemed ready to plunge back into the sea.

He called out to her, "Nita—Nita, it's me—Phil!"

The fog had left him with hardly any voice to call with, but it reached her. Stumbling through the shallow water, she threw herself, soaking wet, into his arms.

Phil never even noticed the sea water streaming off her. He only wanted to go on holding her and kissing her. But at last he took in that she was trying to speak to him, and was saying frantic, incoherent, impossible things.

"Jimmy—they've killed him—he helped me to get away and they shot him—they were going to kill me and he saved me. He had a gun, Phil, when he let me out of the cabin and I thought he was going to kill me, but he told me to jump and swim for it, then when they tried to stop him he started shooting and that horrible man Sid shot him."

"Come on," Phil said, "we're getting out of here."

"But Jimmy—"

"Jimmy's dead, you say. And perhaps that's the best thing for him to be. Come, let's go. They'll be coming after you. And we've got to get you some dry clothes."

She let him lead her towards the foot of the steps.

But as if she could not stop herself, she went on talking.

"It was Sid who knocked you on the head in the Haunted Mill, Phil, and said he'd kill you if I didn't come quietly—at least, it was the other man who said that, the one who was pretending to be the dead man by the mill-wheel."

"Who'd just murdered a girl who he thought was you," Phil said.

"Yes," she said. "They thought I knew about Dr Gavenitz, you see. That's why they were trying to kill me. They thought I'd overheard Jimmy and him arranging to come to Breston together, you see.

"D'you know, he's been kidnapped and hidden here in Breston?" she continued. "But I hadn't heard anything at all. I only heard you making that bet with Jimmy and that's why I came here—I thought somehow I might be able to get you to help me when other people all pretended to think I was insane."

"And so our old friend Jimmy Westlake was the Master Mind in a spy-ring," Phil said. It was lighter now and going up the steps was not as bad as going down, so Phil was hurrying her. "And when I think of all the lunches we've had together . . ."

"Oh, but he wasn't," Nita said.

"He wasn't? Don't tell me that that crazy, pompous uncle of yours, or Aunt Marion . . ."

"No, I don't know who gave the orders," she said. "I don't think Jimmy knew himself. They didn't trust him much. They knew he only worked for them because they had a hold over him—and actually he'd made up his mind to rescue Dr Gavenitz, whatever it cost him. That's why he got you to

Breston. He was like me, he was sure you'd help a person in trouble.''

"Then it must have been Sid," Phil said.

"I think perhaps it was. Sid gave all the orders on the yacht—''

"Sh!"

Two things had happened at that moment. Phil had heard a voice on the cliff-top above him. Also his mind had suddenly cleared so that he knew with absolute certainty who had given the orders for the kidnapping of Dr Gavenitz and that it had not been Sid.

Nita heard the voice and stood still, her body stiffening in terror.

Phil crept softly forward. He reached the top of the cliff-path just as two figures came into view round some twisted thorn-bushes that showed quite clearly now through the lifting mist.

One figure was that of an elderly, stooping man with a drawn face who walked uncertainly as if he could not see properly or were in pain. From photographs that Phil had seen, he recognized Dr Martin Gavenitz. The other, who kept one hand in a pocket that bulged remarkably, was a big, burly man with a heavy, square, ruddy face and great shoulders. Phil knew him at once this time and after the hesitation of only a moment, which was filled with pure panic, assaulted for the third time the policeman whom he had seen mounting the steps of The Yellow Cat.

It was fortunate indeed for Phil that just then Inspector A. with a comforting number of uniformed reinforcements, appeared from behind the thorn-bushes.

There was no miracle about his appearance. Bert Roper, hearing how a man called Courtney had created a disturbance in the hotel, and not wanting to become involved in trouble of any sort himself, had taken the bottle with its mysterious message to the police, and Inspector A. had decided to keep the appointment at Tollard Point.

Later, over an immense breakfast in the Royal Scarlet, Phil said to Nita, "I ought to have realized it at once, of course. What was he doing there, after all, creeping up the back stairs like that? Who had sent for him? It wasn't as if he could have heard Dr Gavenitz moan or your Uncle Hubert laugh. And why, when Inspector A. was questioning me, did he seem to have heard nothing about my having assaulted a member of the police force?"

"Quite so." Though Nita's eyes were shining, her tone, for the moment, was a little dry. "But I do hope that isn't going to become a habit of yours, darling. It'll come so expensive, bailing you out."

NO FLOWERS BY REQUEST

CHAPTER I

Dorothy L. Sayers

"So, OF COURSE, Mummy," said Julia, "Dickie and I hope you will come and make your home with us."

I put on what the children used to call my "tell me another" face.

Julia is one of those daughters who have never given their parents a moment's anxiety, and I am very fond of her and her altogether admirable husband.

But I know exactly what "making my home with them" would be like: unpaid domestic help to Julia; unpaid sewing-woman to Dickie; unpaid nurse to the children; unpaid kennelmaid to two spoilt Pekes and an autocratic Siamese cat. I replied mildly that it seldom worked for two generations to live together.

"But, Mummy, you can't possibly get along on Daddy's tiny pension."

I said I had no intention of doing so. What was in my mind was that, after nearly thirty years (including the better part of two wars) spent in being a strenuous and successful wife and mother, I thought I had earned the right to become, for the first time, the most considered member of a household. Not that my children or my late husband (a charming, though in some ways trying, man) had ever been lacking in affection; but affection is one thing, consideration is quite another.

"What are you going to do then, Mummy?"

I said: "I propose to take a situation as cook-housekeeper."

I will pass over the long series of family expostulations that followed. By the time that well-reasoned letters had arrived from Willie in Edinburgh, Marjorie in California and my sister Maud in Nairobi, I had settled up my affairs, found a tenant for the house, and was sitting in the same register office (which still manages somehow to carry on) where I had so often interviewed exacting cooks, incompetent lady-helps, untrained young women with lipstick and a high value for themselves, and daily charladies reluctantly prepared to oblige.

Only this time I sat on the right side of the table, and was offering my wares upon a sellers' market. It was new and enjoyable.

I was not without sympathy for the would-be employers I turned down—after all, I had been there myself. But it all sounded just like my own suburban home, only duller: and I wanted a change. The more money, outings, sitting-rooms, gadgets and TV they offered, the more difficult I found myself becoming. It was therefore quite a stimulating change when the procession of distracted females was interrupted by a

distracted middle-aged man, who began with re-
freshing candour:

"Good afternoon, Mrs—um—ah—Merton. I'm
afraid I'm on an absolutely hopeless errand. I'm
trying to find a cookhousekeeper for a family of four
in the depths of the country. Invalid wife, ex-RAF
nephew with a game leg, niece and self: no children,
no dogs, no entertaining, no town within miles, no
neighbours, no mod-con. Don't suppose you'd look
at it for a moment."

I said that I could not possibly consider outdoor-
sanitation.

He laughed. "It isn't as bad as that. Company's
water, electricity and some rather inferior local gas.
And there's a village of sorts—only there's nothing
to do in it. I mean, no cinema, no proper shops, and
nowhere to get one's perm set. Of course," he
added, more cheerfully, "I could always run you
over to Kilchester."

I informed him that my hair waved naturally.

He grinned disarmingly. "Does it? Congratula-
tions. As our daily says, it looks almost as good as
artificial."

I noted the presence of the "daily". And I think it
was at that moment I fell for it. That grin came out
of the top drawer. Also, it came out in conversation
that Mr Carringford was a commercial artist, and
had illustrated a lot of stories I'd read in magazines.
I remembered the illustrations because they were
lively and full of character, and he seemed always to
have read the story before doing the pictures.

So after the remote situation, and lack of amenities and the local gas had been allowed for in the
wages (he drove a nice, sensible bargain, being ac-

customed to dealing with editors) and I had conceded something on account of having never been in a situation before (which, as he rightly said, would make me more tiresome about taking orders instead of giving them), and after I had shown him recommendations from our vicar, and our MP and so on, I said:

"Well, now it's my turn. Did you have a cook-housekeeper before and, if so, why did she leave?"

He said: "Well, my wife did the cooking till she got ill. And then we had a lady-cook. She wasn't a lady and she couldn't cook, and she left after a row with the nurse. O Lord, I forgot the nurse. That makes five."

"If there's a hospital nurse," said I firmly, "that must be considered, too. They are excellent women, but they make work."

So we considered the nurse. Finally he said:

"You will be looked on as one of the family, of course."

I said I should much prefer to be looked on as a cook-housekeeper.

"I couldn't agree with you more," said he, "but that's what I was told to tell you."

Hallering Old Rectory was the kind of house which you might call an off-white elephant: too large for a private family and too small for an institution to run economically: old enough to be inconvenient and not old enough to be picturesque: half a mile from Hallering village in one direction, a mile from Thorpe railway station in the other, and about five minutes' walk, panting walk uphill, from a bus-route which functioned, rather irregularly, every two hours.

It was built of grey stone, in a square, uncompromising shape, and was surrounded on three sides by an acre or so of rather overgrown garden. Its front windows looked out, over a short shrubby drive and a rough lawn, to a piece of broken wall and a porch which were the sole remains of Hallering Old Church.

The New Church—an unattractive specimen of Victorian Gothic—had been erected at the far end of the village, whither, some time in the present century, the Rector had thankfully pursued it, and there settled down in a pleasant reconditioned cottage of manageable size.

Marcus Carringford, who met me at the station in a pre-war car—solid as to the engine, but battered as to the coachwork—explained all this rather apologetically as we chirped and rattled up the drive.

"We've only had it about eighteen months, and it's still in a bit of a mess. It had been empty for I don't know how long. Joy!"

The last word was not an explosion of thanksgiving but a loudly bellowed summons, which brought out from behind the shrubbery a hefty young blonde in breeches.

"This is Joy Barnslow, who is nobly endeavouring to make our wilderness blossom. Joy, behold Mrs Merton, the captive of my bow and spear. You'll find the hens in the boot."

This explained various squawkings which had accompanied our progress, and which I had taken to be something wrong with the springs.

Miss Barnslow said "How d'you do?" to me, adding in the same breath, with perhaps a touch of resentment as she wiped the sweat from her forehead, that Mrs Deane was reading a book in the garden and Trent had gone out. She then dived into the boot and strode off abruptly, with a crateful of hens in each hand.

"Not in your department," said Mr Carringford, with a twinkle. "Five only in family as stated. She lives in the village. Her father's the local vet. Good sorts, both of them." He seized my suitcases, pushed open the front door, which badly needed painting, and ushered me through a square hall into a sitting-room at the back. "Sit down, won't you?" he said. "I'll go and hunt up Philippa."

The room, which was pleasantly though shabbily furnished, and agreeably filled with flowers, looked out upon a mixed kind of garden. Vegetables and fruit-trees were flanked by herbaceous borders running down to a tarred fence at the end, where a curtain of giant convolvulus, drooping over a mass of mallow and foxglove, borage and rosebay willow-herb, suggested that Miss Barnslow had not yet got round to the task of civilizing this corner of the estate.

Neither, I was glad to see, had she as yet ejected from the borders the old sweet-scented Provence roses (which I refuse to call cabbage-roses in spite of what Shakespeare says) in favour of those corseted modern varieties which are all shape and no smell. I was gazing out of the window, thinking that it all looked rather pleasant in the summer sunshine, when a woman's voice said just behind me:

"Good afternoon, Mrs Merton. I'm Philippa Deane."

I was stupidly startled, because she had come in

as quietly as a ghost, and when I turned to face her I
was startled again, though in rather a different way.

She was about twenty-eight, I suppose—a slender,
elegant body, very simply dressed in a figured black
and grey frock, moving with the effortless ease of
flowing water, and surmounted, as it swam out of
the shadows of the room, by a beautiful and perfectly expressionless mask.

It was a face from which all life and spontaneity
seemed to have been drained out—no, that is not the
word—deliberately and ruthlessly withdrawn.

It said: If I have feelings, you shall never guess
what they are. The impression of determined secrecy
stamped on mouth and forehead was somehow en-
hanced by the dark, shining hair, matt-white skin,
and the dark eyes in which the iris could scarcely be
distinguished from the pupil.

I was suddenly reminded of a fairy story that
frightened me as a child—all about Somebody the
Sorceress.

Meanwhile I was exchanging commonplace greet-
ings with Mrs Deane, who offered to show me to my
room. As we started to climb the stairs a uniformed
nurse rustled briskly across the hall, shot a glance at
me which said as clearly as print, "And how much
trouble will this woman be, I wonder," and disappeared through a door at the far end.

"Nurse Cutler," said Mrs Deane to me. "My
aunt sleeps on the ground floor because of her heart.
She rests in the afternoon; she'll see you after tea.
That is my uncle's room, and my cousin Trent's is
just beyond. Mine is down the other passage and
your bedroom and sitting-room are here."

She opened the door, remarked that her uncle had

brought up all my things, informed me that the bath-room was at the end of the corridor, and hoped I should be comfortable, all with perfect politeness and without the faintest expression of interest.

I thanked her, and said it all looked very nice. She then left me to take off my hat and unpack, saying that she would return in half an hour to show me the kitchen premises, unless I would like to rest a little first.

I thanked her again, and said that I should prefer to take up my duties at once.

"Very well," she said, "though if you are tired, I dare say Nurse would make tea for us. Mrs Hutchinson only comes in the mornings."

I replied that I felt perfectly capable of making tea, and she drifted away. I noted that, as far as household duties were concerned, Mrs Deane appeared to be a passenger in the boat, and resolved that Nurse Cutler should never, if I could help it, be asked to put herself out on my account.

Returning with admirable punctuality at the expiration of the half-hour, Mrs Deane led me to the kitchen, which was roomy, though rather dark, and contained a gas-stove, remarkably dirty, and a dresser chaotically piled with crockery and cooking implements.

Mrs Deane did not come in, but contented herself with standing at the door and saying that the scullery, pantry and larder were beyond and she hoped I should be able to find what I wanted. She then departed, after mentioning that they usually had tea about half-past four.

It did not take me five minutes to register a vow

that before I was twenty-four hours older I would
have that kitchen turned inside out.

My predecessor (the one who was neither lady nor
cook) must have been a singularly untidy woman,
and I suspected that an interregnum of unaided Mrs
Hutchinson had done nothing to straighten out the
confusion she had left behind her.

I discovered a set of tea-things on the draining-
board, an inlaid Sheraton tray in the larder, a trussed
fowl and a trug full of sprouts in the pantry, a jug of
milk in the china-cupboard and some potatoes under
the sink.

The butter eluded me for some time: but eventu-
ally I tracked it down in the meat-safe, which also
contained some cakes on an enamel plate, and a
bowl of cooked fish-heads, thoughtfully ticketed CAT—
lest, I suppose, I should be tempted to eat them
myself.

I had just found the sugar in a canister labelled
SPICES, and was shaking various other containers in
the hope of coming upon the tea, when Mr Carringford's head came suddenly through the window and
asked how I was getting on.

He seemed to know his way about the kitchen, for
he at once directed me to the right quarter—a biscuit
tin on the scullery shelf—and explained that the
family all drank China, except his wife, who liked
"sergeant-major's tea, Indian, sweet, and strong"
—which was made for her in her own room by
Nurse Cutler.

He then apologized for the absence of a refrigera-
tor, an electric sweeper, and various other things

which he had "not yet succeeded in affording", and showed me where the table-linen was kept.

I remarked that he was admirably domesticated. This simple pleasantry seemed to disconcert him. He mumbled that his wife had been in poor health for a long time, and his niece wasn't much given that way—

At that moment an acid voice somewhere outside inquired only too plainly, "Well! has the new incompetent arrived?" and somebody else said, "Shush!" Mr Carringford, with an air between embarrassment and relief, said, "Oh dear! that's Trent," and escaped, shutting the door very firmly behind him, before I could ask whether I was expected to have tea with the family.

Nurse Cutler, who came in presently in quest of boiling water, supplied the answer. She carried a tray with two teapots—one for herself and one for her patient—and gave her orders for thin bread-and-butter, cake, sliced lemon and milk as though she were a travelling Briton in a foreign café, determined to stand no nonsense.

She was a good-looking, youngish woman with red hair, a bust, and (I thought) a temper when roused.

"They'll want you to have meals with them," she said. "It gives them someone to talk to. I'd as soon eat in a morgue myself. Not but what my old girl's tiresome enough—kidneys mostly are. But you can't always choose your patient: you can choose your company."

I was starting across the hall with the tea-things when Mr Carringford (who seemed a helpful man, as men go) appeared from somewhere and carried them into the sitting-room for me.

Mrs Deane was there on the sofa, doing some embroidery. She did not bestir herself, and I gathered that I was expected to pour out. As I was taking my place at the tea-table, a young man limped in, supporting himself on a stick, and was introduced as Mr Trent Carringford.

He had evidently been strong and good-looking before the flying accident which had crippled him; but his left leg was badly distorted, and the whole of that side of his face was terribly scarred; neither did he appear to have the full use of his left arm. I learned afterwards that his machine had caught fire, and he had been badly burned all down that side before they were able to drag him out. By some miracle he had kept the sight of both eyes, but the left side of his mouth had acquired a permanent twist which was disconcerting—you found it difficult to tell, till you came to know him, whether he was smiling or sneering.

CHAPTER II

Dorothy L. Sayers

I WILL PASS over the conversation, which was devoted to commonplaces, and from which I learned only that Trent Carringford was engaged in writing a book—something historical, apparently, about witchcraft in King James I's time—and that the cat for whom the fish in the larder was destined was an animal of independent habits, called Sennacherib.

He was probably "out rabbiting" in the paddock and would in due course present himself in the kitchen and ask for his supper, but I must not allow him to make a nuisance of himself.

When we had finished tea Trent volunteered to help with the washing-up, and Mr Carringford sent his niece to ask whether her aunt was ready to see me.

I made no objection to the washing-up proposal—for one thing, I had determined from the start to let myself be "considered", and besides, I am all for making men take their due share of the work.

* * *

We were getting along very well—Mr Carringford washing, Trent drying (managing very neatly, in spite of his disabilities), and I putting the things away in what I had decided should be their proper places, when Mrs Deane came to the kitchen door and said in a tone of some alarm: "Uncle Marcus!" Mr Carringford went out to her rather hastily and they conferred for a little time in the hall. Trent's damaged face was to me inscrutable, but I thought he looked worried.

Presently his father came back and said: "Trent—ring up Grayling"; and then to me: "I'm afraid my wife is not so well, and won't be able to see you just at present." Then he, too, went away.

Having had some experience of illness I promptly put the kettle on to boil; and Nurse Cutler, coming in shortly afterwards with two hot-water bottles, was so surprised by my forethought that she actually commended and thanked me.

She added, however, that in any decently-run household there would be a gas-ring in the patient's bedroom. I replied that I would try to arrange for one; whereon she bounced out with the bottles, saying only: "And high time, too."

It was not I who opened the door for Dr Grayling; but he must have come almost as soon as he was summoned, for when—after exploring the cupboards more thoroughly and cleaning some of the worst grease from the stove—I presently emerged from the kitchen, he was just crossing the hall with Mr Carringford on his way out. He was a pleasant, energetic-looking man of about forty, and was saying with some emphasis: "I agree, it's not at all satisfactory. Perhaps you would like—"

Mr Carringford was frowning gravely, and they went into a muttered consultation on the door-mat. I opened the sitting-room door.

Mr Trent and Mrs Deane were there, but they did not notice me. Mrs Deane was sitting near the window, and for the first time I saw her face with some expression on it. And that was fear—plain, ugly fear. She said: "I can't stand it, Trent—not again." His back was towards me. He said, in an odd, hard tone, "Then hadn't you better clear out?"

I thought that if anybody cleared out it had better be me. I had intended to ask about the sweet, but decided that I would make up something with some tins of fruit that I had discovered. So I made a tactful retirement, shutting the door quietly.

Some time later, Nurse Cutler arrived to prepare some meat essence. She said that her patient had had a nasty attack—a fainting fit—but was better now. So I roasted the chicken and said no more. Dinner was not exactly a hilarious meal, but they all, including Nurse Cutler, seemed to be cheered up by my cooking.

Fortunately, when Mrs Hutchinson turned up next morning, she proved to be a florid, cheerful woman—a natural slattern, but an energetic worker under direction. She entered with enthusiasm into the idea of turning out the kitchen, feeling evidently that here was a job which called for all her mettle.

She talked, indeed, as fast as she worked. Though I refused to listen to her opinion of my predecessor, I could not help learning that Mr Carringford wouldn't have nobody dust his studio not if it was ever so; that Mrs Deane was his wife's niece and Mr Trent his own nephew (their own son had been killed in the war); that Mrs Deane wasn't proud, though she wouldn't never set foot in the kitchen, and had given her (Mrs Hutchinson) a sweetly pretty scarf last Christmas . . .

Also, that everybody had been expecting Miss Barnslow's engagement to Dr Grayling, but it seemed to have gone off somehow; that Mrs C. wasn't Mr C.'s class, and some people said she used to drink before she got ill, but that was afore they come here and she (Mrs Hutchinson) was never one to gossip; that Mr Trent's room was full of 'orrible pictures and books about poison, and a nasty black 'ed on the wall what would give you quite a turn . . .

"And what would that be, I wonder?" said Mrs Hutchinson, rattling a tin which was conspicuously labelled POISON; moth-balls, maybe, or them tablets for slugs. It proved, however, to contain nothing worse than a number of bone buttons.

It is surprising how much rubbish can accumulate, even in eighteen months, when no attempt is made to keep order. When all the identifiable substances had been put in their right places and properly labelled, there remained a pile of empty or half-empty bottles, tins, cartons and boxes which covered the kitchen table, and were only fit for burning.

I am always particular about nameless white powders, and dribs and drabs of things from the chemist, calling themselves simply "The Lotion", or "The mixture as before". They might be absolutely anything. When we had finished making our collection,

I showed it to Mr Carringford and asked his permission to get rid of it.

"Good God!" he said. "Yes, of course, burn the lot. I wonder we haven't all been—" He broke off suddenly, and burst out laughing, as though a load had been taken off his mind. "I'm going into Kilchester for the fish," he said. "Is there anything else you'd like me to get?"

I mentioned Nurse's gas-ring and a few other things, which he promised to fetch. "And I'm glad to say," he added, "that my wife is much better today, and would like to see you as soon as you're free."

I must say that I did not take to Mrs Carringford. I got the impression that young Mr Carringford must have married his model in haste and repented at leisure. She had the remains of remarkable good looks, but her face was puffy and peevish, and her voice common.

When I got there, Mrs Deane was arranging a bowl of flowers on the low window-sill, where Sennacherib—a stout gentleman in a very handsome dress-suit—was lying majestically asleep, with his chin on a Georgian walnut tea-caddy.

Mrs Carringford asked me a lot of questions—many of them, to my mind, impertinently personal, but I suppose she had nothing much to think about, lying there ill all day, and a new housekeeper was a distraction for her.

I patiently told her where and of whom I was born, where I had lived, what my husband's business had been, how many children I had, what my means were, and why I had decided to take a situation.

"And what did your husband die of?" was the next. "Not poisoned by your cooking, I hope?" And she went off into a hoot of very unpleasant laughter. Mrs Deane exclaimed reproachfully, "Oh, Aunt Eleanor!" I restrained myself, and replied quietly that my husband had been killed in a motor-accident.

"Then he was luckier than some," said Mrs Carringford. She gave another hoot of her unkind laughter but after a moment she put out her hand, with a gesture of apology, to her niece. "Never mind, Philippa; I'm on your side," she said.

CHAPTER III

E. C. R. Lorac

I WAS WRITING to my daughter Julia—the sort of letter which would assure her that I was comfortably settled. But I just *had* to get some air.

As I strolled slowly along the rather tangled herbaceous border, I tried to sort out my own sense of unease, the reason for the impulse which had flashed across my mind, "I can't stand this: there's something wrong here . . ."

The plain fact was that every member of the household seemed odd. "Odd. Queer. Peculiar . . ." Those were the words my generation had been taught to use: today they said Pathological . . . Neurotic . . . Maladjusted.

Somewhere from below the surface of my mind a phrase I'd learnt in childhood swam up: ". . . the unruly wills and affections of sinful men . . ."

Marcus Carringford: he was kind, sociable, laughter-loving; successful in his own profession; and he was married to a very unpleasant, ill-bred woman who had a singularly nasty tongue.

I remembered her cackle after she had said: "He was luckier than some." (And it was my husband's death she'd been talking about.) Why had Marcus Carringford brought his wife to live in this remote country place, when she was so obviously an urban product?

Streets were her line of country: streets, shops, cinemas, cafés—not rutted lanes and "immemorial elm". And had my eyes deceived me when I passed Mr Carringford and Nurse Cutler on the landing last night?

Here I gave myself a mental shake—this was charwoman level—but I couldn't forget the complacency of Nurse Cutler's voice when she had said "These kidney cases—they often go off into a coma. . ." (Quite true, of course.)

Philippa Deane was a beautiful young woman— and what on earth was she doing in this household? Any girl with looks and a figure like hers could take her choice of jobs in London—receptionist, model, mannequin, air-hostess. Mrs Deane . . . no mention of a husband: and she had that withdrawn, remote look . . .

I bent to pull up a flourishing groundsel, whose gossamer seeds were floating about.

Having screwed the thing up in my hand, I was immediately faced with the problem of disposing of it and I walked to the corner of the garden where I had noticed a compost heap and bonfire behind some wattle fencing: there was a potting-shed as well.

The door of the latter was open and as I glanced in

I couldn't help seeing that Trent Carringford and Joy
Barnslow were both inside the shed, leaning against
the potting bench, their heads very close together.

I should very much have preferred to walk past as
though I hadn't seen them, but Trent's eye caught
mine. I called: "What a lovely afternoon," and
would have walked on, but Trent replied:

"Lovely, isn't it? So nice for a little walk in the
garden."

He came outside and stood by the door, so that he
was between me and Joy Barnslow and went on:
"Been doing a little weeding? Are you an expert at
gardening as well as cooking?"

I couldn't tell from his face whether he was sneering or smiling, but I have very quick ears: I knew
that behind him, in the darkness of the shed, Joy
Barnslow was crying.

Suddenly she emerged from the shed, pushing him
aside; she had got herself in hand now, and though
her face was flushed she was no longer crying.

Trent limped off at a faster pace than I should
have thought him capable of, and Joy said unhappily: "He's so bitter."

"My dear, can you wonder?" I replied. "When a
lad has suffered like that and been half crippled it'd
be astonishing if he weren't bitter. And now tell me
what I'm to do with these wretched weeds: I feel
such a fool walking about with a fistful of seeding
groundsel."

She laughed at that, tremulously, but laughing all
the same.

She took a fork and lifted the top layer of half-
burnt weeds and I plunged my seeding pests into the
ashes, saying: "I see you burn some household rub-

bish, too—that isn't all garden rubbish, is it? I'm glad to know that. Disposal of household refuse can be quite a problem in the country, when the dust-carts don't come round very frequently.''

She looked up at me in a startled way and then rammed the cold ashes down again, as she said quickly: ''Rubbish from the house is burnt in the incinerator in the old wash-house. This is all garden rubbish—you've no idea what fantastic things you find buried in old gardens; skeletons of perished pets to skeletons of Victorian corsets, and bottles galore, broken and otherwise. Bottle necks seem indestructible.''

I patted her shoulder: ''All right, my dear. I think I can understand: you see I've been turning out the kitchen—but it's much easier to reduce a kitchen to order than a garden.''

I spoke with no ulterior thought in my mind, but a scared look flashed over Joy's face for a second. ''It must have been awful,'' she said. ''The last Treasure was a mental defective—and she *would* bury empty bottles in my compost heap. Oh dear, you must think we're a very queer lot of people.''

I repeated this observation to myself as I walked back to the kitchen to put my sweet peas in water and to get the tea. Odd . . . Queer . . . Peculiar . . . Pathological . . . Neurotic . . . Maladjusted . . .

And then Sennacherib came and rubbed round my ankles.

Something in his expression told me that he was a very affronted cat; somebody had disturbed him, turned him off his comfortable sunny window-sill in Mrs Carringford's room.

I picked him up to stroke him and found his coat

was almost electric under my fingers—or else I was
shivering, quite unreasonably.

After tea I finished off my letter to Julia: I found
myself incapable of adding anything to it except that
the weather was perfect. I had meant to describe the
garden, with the lovely wild flowers by the fence at
the end, but that part of the garden was now con-
nected in my mind with Joy Barnslow's unhappy
face. Why had she been crying, why did she look
scared?

A sharp knock on the door cut across my thoughts.
I called "Come in" and Nurse Cutler appeared: she
was no longer in uniform but in a very smart black
suit, cut to reveal her generous lines, and immacu-
late nylons.

"Sorry to intrude," she said abruptly. "It's my
evening off duty, and God knows I need it. I wondered if you'd be kind enough to look in at my
patient after dinner . . ."

"I'm sorry," I said. "A nurse must have her
off-duty hours respected—but I'm afraid I'm not the
answer. Surely Mr Carringford is the right person to
be with your patient while you are out?"

"Him?" Her voice spoke volumes.

She slammed the door behind her and I heard her
high heels tapping noisily down the corridor.

CHAPTER IV

E. C. R. Lorac

I WENT DOWN to the kitchen and got busy with cooking supper. I was just getting busy with the eggs when the niece, Philippa Deane, came in. I felt more than a little exasperated. Perhaps my face showed it, for she apologized very politely for interrupting, adding: "It's just that I'm so worried I felt I had to talk to someone, and you look so sensible and well balanced, Mrs Merton, it's comforting even to look at you."

"I'm sure that's nicely meant," I replied, beating the eggs steadily, "but I didn't really come here to be a comfort to anybody, except in the sense of providing good meals and an orderly household."

She didn't reply, and I think she would have gone out of the room without speaking again, but unfortunately I looked up and caught the expression on her face, and she looked so wretched that I put the basin down and said: "Tell me what's worrying you—sometimes just talking helps."

"Oh, indeed it does!" she cried, a faint flush creeping up into the cold pallor of her face (and what a lovely face it was). "It's about Mrs Carringford. Nurse Cutler has gone out and I'm sure Mrs Carringford is ill—I mean worse than she generally is. She looks dreadful to me."

"Well then—ring up the doctor," I cried. "Don't hesitate. What are doctors for?"

"It isn't so simple as you think," she said unhappily. "Dr Grayling is away this evening and Dr Barr takes his surgery for him and is on call if needed: but Mrs Carringford can't bear Dr Barr—she simply loathes him."

As though in a flash of clairvoyance I saw a number of things with rather dreadful clarity. Nurse Cutler had gone out on pleasure bent. That Marcus Carringford had gone to share Nurse's jaunt . . .

Mrs Carringford had taken a turn for the worse, and her niece was left in charge on the evening when Dr Grayling was not available.

All too clearly I remembered that revealing cry of Philippa Deane's which I had overheard . . . "Not again . . . I couldn't bear it."

I cut up the bacon, fitted the pastry to the round dish and assembled my pie with a speed and lack of care most unlike my usual habits. Mrs Deane sat crumbling the odd fragments of pastry while I put my pie in the oven. Then I said: "What you really want is for me to ring up Dr Barr—is that it?"

"I should be very grateful if you would, Mrs Merton, but in case you think I'm just making a fuss, won't you come and look at Mrs Carringford? I expect you know much more about illness than I do."

With a feeling that a concerted effort was being made to involve me in responsibility for the invalid, I followed Philippa Deane into her aunt's bedroom: indeed it seemed impossible to refuse.

The room was very dim—the curtains were drawn over the windows—and only a faint diffused light showed me Mrs Carringford's face. She lay on her back, asleep. I listened to her respiration; it was slow but not laboured. Very carefully I laid my hand on her forehead, which was unhealthily damp, and felt the pulse in her temple.

I left the room quietly and Philippa followed me, looking like a ghost herself.

"What do you think?" she asked anxiously.

"I can't judge, because I don't know anything about the patient," I rejoined coldly. "Do you know if Nurse gave her a sedative before she went out?"

"I don't know. She just said: 'She's quite quiet now. I should leave her for a bit.'"

"Then it didn't look as though Nurse were worrying," I replied. "Nevertheless, since you are anxious, I will ring up Dr Barr. Do you know his number?"

She glanced at her watch. "He'll have left the surgery and got home by now," she said. "His number's Clanton 92. He lives about ten miles from here."

It was a woman's voice that answered the 'phone, and an irritable woman at that. "Can I speak to Dr Barr?" I asked.

"Dr Barr has been called out. Can you leave a message, please?"

"This is Mrs Carringford's housekeeper speaking from Hallering Old Rectory. Nurse Cutler is out, and

I am very anxious about Mrs Carringford. Can I get in touch with Dr Barr?''

"Quite impossible," retorted the irritable voice. "He is out at a maternity case up at Long Meadham. . . . I shouldn't worry too much. Mrs Carringford has given people frights several times before—quite unnecessarily. Just keep her warm and quiet. As for another doctor—Dr Blakeley's the nearest, but he's over twenty miles from Hallering. I'll give Dr Barr your message when he comes in.''

She rang off, and I was aware of Philippa Deane hovering behind me.

"Now it's no use worrying," I said. "Nurse will be in by ten o'clock. By the way, I suppose Mr Carringford will be in to supper at eight?"

"I don't know, he didn't say," she replied. "I'm sorry, but this house is like that sometimes.''

"If Mrs Carringford were my aunt, I certainly shouldn't like to leave her alone as she is now," I replied. Then, feeling I'd been rather harsh, I added, "You go and sit with her now, and I'll have my supper when the pie is cooked. Then you can come down and have your supper in peace and I'll sit with her."

She went back to Mrs Carringford's room without a word.

Marcus Carringford came in at half-past nine. His wife was still asleep.

Nurse Cutler came in twenty minutes later—and then things began to happen: she stormed helplessly over the telephone. Dr Barr was still out, Dr Grayling's whereabouts unknown.

Nurse sent Marcus Carringford off in the car to

run Dr Grayling to earth, and then told me to come and help her in the sick-room. The patient was much colder now.

We packed her round with fresh hot bottles, and Nurse injected a shot of coramine. When I had seen her at seven o'clock, Mrs Carringford was lying flat. After supper she was half sitting up, propped by pillows, to ease her breathing, I suppose—it was very laboured.

It was just before midnight when she died, five minutes before Marcus Carringford returned with Dr Grayling.

I went to the kitchen and made some tea. Mrs Carringford was no concern of mine, but I admit I was appalled. Picture after picture flashed across my mind and wild conjectures with them. I was just going to empty the teapot when Nurse Cutler came in, looking curiously deflated, colourless, limp

"For God's sake give me a cuppa . . . He's sealed the room . . . says he can't understand it. That means a PM. I wish I'd never taken the case on."

She broke off, and then asked abruptly, "Was it you who sat her up against the pillows?"

"Indeed not," I replied. "I didn't touch her."

"Funny—Mrs Deane says she didn't either. Oh, Lord, I don't know . . . Looks as though we're all in it together."

"What on earth do you mean, Nurse?" I demanded indignantly.

"She was all right when I went out," she said obstinately, "and now she's dead . . . Give me some more sugar in this, it tastes frightful. I like Indian tea, really, not this sick-making China muck.''

"Well, I'll make you another pot," I suggested.

"No go, dear. My Indian tea's in a tin in her room, and the room's locked up as I told you." She added, thoughtfully: "She won't have any further need for that precious special tea of hers in the antique caddy—will she?''

CHAPTER V

Gladys Mitchell

THE POST-MORTEM examination had the most frightful consequences. Mrs Carringford had been poisoned. To my horror, I had to attend the inquest, but the matter was so grave that after the body had been identified by poor Marcus Carringford and the medical evidence had been taken, the proceedings were adjourned.

The following days were like a nightmare. We had to put up with the police—that one had expected, of course—but worse, to my mind, than any police was the general atmosphere of suspicion, distrust and fear.

As day succeeded day I could not help becoming aware that I was being used as a foil by every member of the household. If I had felt that I was being used as a confidante it would have been different, but it was not a bit like that. I was being used as a go-between.

The first to come was Philippa Deane, on the

excuse of asking whether I had any stale bread with which she could feed the birds.

"I suppose you'll leave us as soon as the situation is cleared up," she said, accepting the heel of the loaf with a nod of thanks. "I wish you need not, but I hardly think you'd care to stay on, would you?"

I looked at her in surprise. It may seem odd to say so, but the idea of leaving the Carringfords' house had never occurred to me.

"I have no plans at present," I replied. "This is no time, in my opinion, to think of myself."

"Oh, but we've all got to, haven't we?" she demanded. "There's this wretched inquest to come up again. I've tried to sound Tom Grayling, but he won't give away a thing. Have you had a talk with him yet?"

"Well, no, but, then, I scarcely know Dr Grayling." (Tom, I thought to myself. So that's the way the wind blows, does it!)

"I suppose not, but that's all the more reason why he might let out to you the things he's keeping from us. The inquest, so far, was so unsatisfactory."

"I don't see that it was unsatisfactory," I interrupted quietly.

"Well, the doctors didn't agree, did they?"

"They agreed that Mrs Carringford had been suffering from digitalin poisoning. The only thing they did not agree on was whether the digitalin was sufficient to cause death. At least, that's how I understood it."

"Well, I want to know what Tom really thinks," she insisted. "If he—if he should tell you anything, I wish you'd let me know. I have a right to the knowledge—a much better right than you imagine."

But little as I could conceive of Dr Grayling con-
fiding in me or, indeed, in anyone else, if I had
summed him up rightly—I was making no promises.

Just then Joy Barnslow went past my kitchen window, and Philippa Deane, who had been crumbling
the stale bread nervously on to Mrs Hutchinson's
nice, clean floor, started for the door with the remains of the loaf. Scarcely had she disappeared
when Joy came back and tapped at the kitchen
window.

"What do you want for lunch and dinner?" she
asked.

"Come round," I replied.

"I say," she said, in the forthcoming, militant
voice which she used in speaking to Trent, Philippa
and myself, "that woman and her bird-seed! Why
does she keep on watching me while I'm at work?
She stands there fiddling about with bits of bread
and chopped-up fat meat and things, and pretends to
be feeding the birds, but it's me she's got her cats'
eyes on. What's she up to?"

"I'm sure she isn't up to anything," I answered.
"She needs an occupation, something to take her
mind off things, I think. She is very highly-strung
and nervous, and the ideas of having the police in
the house, and of being questioned, and of having to
look forward to a resumption of the inquest have
been preying on her mind."

"As well they might!" retorted Joy.

"Whatever do you mean?" I inquired. She flushed,
bit her lip and looked obstinate.

"Just what I say," she answered.

Now my bump of curiosity is strong, and I was

dying for her to tell me what she meant, but a sense of caution refused to allow me to question her.

"You are asking about the vegetables for lunch and dinner," I said. "Runner beans and potatoes will do for lunch, and for dinner we had better have peas, if there are enough. Can you manage some raspberries today?"

"Yes, certainly. And now, look here, if you wouldn't mind dropping a hint to Philippa Deane that I can do my work without any supervision from her, I'd be more than grateful."

But again I was careful to make no promises. All the same, I thought it not a bad idea to keep an eye on our bird fancier. That there was a rift between the two girls was obvious, but whether it had been made mutually or only by Joy Barnslow I was not so certain. There were wheels within wheels in the relationships. Of this, of course, I had been aware from the first. I recollected my earlier thoughts about certain members of the household. Odd. Queer. Peculiar. Pathological. Neurotic. Maladjusted. Scared.

As I prepared the lunch in the comparatively short interval of peace allotted to me daily while Mrs Hutchinson "did the upstairs", I turned over in my mind all that I knew or guessed concerning the two girls.

Joy, I realized, was fundamentally a thwarted, unhappy person. I put her age as around twenty-five. I was not prepared to believe that her ingenuous, rough-skinned, "open-air" face concealed secrets which could be damaging if they were known. She could not be afraid of her employer, for Marcus was no slave-driver: very far from it. He was only too anx-

ious to let everything slide which did not interfere
with him and his own work.

I had seen a good deal of the latter, for there were
always rough sketches as well as finished illustrations lying about in the room he used as a den, and
very early in my term of office as cook-housekeeper
he had begged me not to let Mrs Hutchinson loose in
there.

"She means well," he said, "but her only idea of
'straightening-up', as she calls it, is to put everything where I can't find it. I don't mind if the room
never gets done at all, provided that my stuff is left
alone."

I could not leave it at that, so I promised to do the
den myself on any day that was most convenient to
him. He seemed extraordinarily pleased when I said
this, and thanked me more heartily than the occasion
warranted.

"I'm quite accustomed to young men and their
untidy ways," I said, feeling somewhat embarrassed
by his pleasure and the warmth with which he ex-
pressed it.

He turned away and then suddenly turned back.
"Young man!" he said with a laugh that seemed
slightly bitter. "Don't you know, Mrs Merton, that
I'm fifty?"

He gave me a queer look, and went out without
another word. Mrs Hutchinson had taken kindly to
the idea that I was to do some of her work for her.

"Some of it's so rude," she informed me. "He
draws them young ladies first, and draws the clo'es
on 'em afterwards. I'm sure my Bert wouldn't like it
if he knowed some of the sights I've seen in that
there room."

"Mr Carringford has to get the anatomy right," I pointed out, although I must confess I was a little startled by her remark. Could there be something pathological about a commercial artist who had this passion for nudes? I dismissed the thought and duly cleaned, swept and dusted the den and looked with frank curiosity at any drawings left lying about.

"No children, and an invalid, fretful wife," I thought. "Poor Mr Carringford! Poor, handsome, frustrated Marcus, my dear!"

CHAPTER VI

Gladys Mitchell

I WENT TO look for Mrs Hutchinson. I wanted her to do the vegetables. On my way, duster in hand, I met Nurse Cutler.

"Oh," she said, staring spitefully at the duster in my hand. "I notice that if you're above doing nurse's work you have no objection to helping out that charlady! Tastes differ, I must say!" She was going on past me down the stairs, but I stopped her.

"One moment, Nurse Cutler," I said. "There is something I want to ask you." I could not swear to it, but it seemed to me that something very much like panic fled, as it were, into her eyes.

"Oh?" she said.

"It is about Mrs Carringford's death." I went on. "You remember that you asked me whether it was I who set her up against the pillows, and I told you that I did not?"

"I remember," she said, and the panic fled from her eyes again, leaving her as she had looked on the night of the death—deflated, colourless and limp. "I told you that Mrs Deane said the same thing, and so she did. Why? What makes you bring that up again? It couldn't have had any bearing."

"That isn't what you said at the time," I reminded her. "You said—I remember your exact words because they sounded to me so extraordinary unless you possess knowledge which has not been revealed to the rest of us—you said, 'Looks as though we're all in it together.' You remember?"

"I don't know what you're getting at, Mrs Merton," she retorted. "Perhaps you'll say straight out what you mean!"

"But that is just what I'm asking *you* to do, Nurse Cutler," I returned. "Whatever you meant by those words, they have a strange ring now that there is all this mystery over Mrs Carringford's death, and that the inquest has had to be adjourned so that the police can collect further evidence. What exactly were you getting at?—and whom did you mean by 'all'?"

Her eyes flickered away from mine. All her cheap arrogance was gone, and it was a worried, frightened woman who stood before me.

"You don't know what I know," she muttered. I held her eyes for a full half-minute.

"It is no business of mine," I replied. "Anything you know you ought to tell the police. As for this . . ." I flicked the clean duster I was holding . . . "What I do in the way of housework I do of my own choice."

"Of course, Mrs Merton," she answered. She still sounded completely deflated. I let her go, but I was worried. She knew something, probably because of her profession, which was hidden from the rest of us. I could not help wondering what it was. It was something to do with the fact that Mrs Carringford had been sitting up when (or just before) she died.

I racked my brains, but the fact is that, apart from childish complaints, such as chicken-pox and measles, I have little knowledge of illness, and her sly innuendoes really meant nothing to me: neither did I propose to question her further. I did not like her, and I did not think she was a good woman. What her private life and private thoughts were I had not the faintest idea.

Only one thing disturbed my mind. What was the matter with Philippa Deane that she seemed so nervous and worried?

This particular query was soon answered, although whether truthfully or not I could not, at that time, tell. Nurse Cutler went on her way downstairs, and I ascended to flush Mrs Hutchinson from her lair. This proved to be my own bedroom, which I had undertaken to keep clean and tidy myself.

"Thank you, Mrs Hutchinson," I said. "The vegetables are in. Perhaps you would go down and do them, and I will finish here."

"Just as you like, dear," she replied. The affectionate terms now used by charwomen, shopgirls and bus conductors will never really become part of my life. To me they always convey the veiled insult implicit in the theory that Jack is as good as his master. Of course he isn't—if he were he would surely be a master on his own account instead of a paid employee.

Anyhow, it *was* as I liked, for she took herself and the carpet-sweeper downstairs while I went into Marcus Carringford's den.

It was in an even worse disorder than usual, but

none of the usual drawings was about. Instead there were papers everywhere—old income-tax demands and receipts, bills (all receipted, as far as I could see) and a lot of torn-up paper which might have been anything.

In the midst of all this mess sat the master of the house. Beside him was a bottle of brandy, and the atmosphere of the room held its own tale.

"I think you had better go to bed," I said severely. "I have come to clear up this workroom."

"Oh, you have?" said he, looking owlish. "See here, my dear, what do you really think happened? About my wife, you know. I can't get anyone to tell me the truth. Now, they all talk to you. What's your honest opinion? Do tell me!"

"I haven't one," I answered, distressed. "And people don't talk to me. They try to talk to one another through me. What do you yourself think?"

"All sorts of things, Mrs Merton. If I had any suspicions I suppose I'd suspect myself, but, you see, I can't quite do that because I know I didn't do it."

"Didn't do what, Mr Carringford?" I was becoming alarmed. In his present state he might utter any indiscretions!

"Didn't poison my wife, you know. Those policemen think I did. I can tell they do. But they're wrong. The real trouble lies between me and my conscience, because, you know, Mrs M., I've thought of it a good many times. Digitalis . . . and with all those fox-gloves down by where little What-Name burns the garden rubbish! Precious Bane, and all that! Do you see what I mean?"

"What I see most clearly is that you'd better go to

bed," I said coldly. "I'll call you when lunch is ready." And with that I steered him from the den.

But I had not the heart to set to work on the room. Something was seriously wrong, and Marcus knew what it was. I flicked around listlessly after he had gone, and then pulled myself together and went down to my kitchen, there to encounter, of all people, young Trent Carringford.

"Sorry to intrude," he said, in his usual half-teasing, half-insulting manner, "but there's something I want your advice on, Nanny Merton."

"I don't know that I am qualified to give advice, Mr Trent," I answered. I felt I'd had enough for one morning.

"I know, Nanny dear," he went on, taking care, as he always did, poor lad, to keep the better side of his face towards me. "But I think you might help a bloke out. The person I'm worried about is Philippa. She's dead scared over all this hoodoo, and no wonder. I suppose you know her story?"

"Of course I don't. I've only been here a matter of days," I said.

"I thought my late unlamented aunt-by-marriage would have told you. But I want you to know that Philippa had nothing to do with this business. You might let her know that I've told you, and that I'm prepared to stand by her to the last."

"I give no undertaking," I began, but he would not listen.

"The point is that her husband—a cad and a rotter if ever there was one!—died under very suspicious circumstances a short time back. He was poisoned. Fortunately the coroner's jury took the point of view that it was suicide—largely thanks to Tom Grayling's evidence—otherwise Philly might have found herself in Queer Street. So if she seems nervy and a bit beside herself, just remember that she's been here before." His voice was defiant and did not help his argument.

"She's been here before," he repeated.

I could not for the life of me decide whether he was really pleading her cause or putting me on my guard.

CHAPTER VII

Anthony Gilbert

AFTER TRENT HAD gone I went into the dining-room
to see about setting the table for lunch. Someone
was already there. I heard a voice.

"All I can say is, it's not like the murders I'm used
to."

I pushed the door open. Mrs Hutchinson was there
with Nurse Cutler. Before they could recover themselves I inquired crisply, "And what kind of murders are you used to, Mrs Hutchinson?"

She wasn't in the least abashed. "Well, if this 'ad
been one of those detective stories we'd be a lot
further on by now. Why, we've 'ardly started. What
about fingerprints? and motives? and clues?"

"You're talking of fiction," I reminded her. "This
is the truth."

"I never did see much fun in truth," was her
candid rejoinder. "Mind you, if I was the police I
wouldn't be in much doubt."

Nurse Cutler, who had been looking remarkably

uncomfortable, made some excuse and took herself off.

"I like you, dear," said Mrs Hutchinson unexpectedly. "If I didn't, I wouldn't be warning you."

"Warning me against what?"

"In those books I was telling you about it's always the one nobody thinks of who's done it."

"While in real life," I pointed out, setting knives and forks round the table with no assistance from Mrs Hutchinson, "the obvious person is usually guilty."

"That's what I mean. Motive. I know they say the police don't need a motive, but it does help."

"And you know who has a motive?"

"Well, look at it this way. Nobody could pretend Mr Carringford's broken-hearted about his wife. No blame to him, I couldn't stand 'er myself, but all said and done, 'e did marry 'er. And there's another thing— what about the will?"

"Was there one?"

Mrs Hutchinson stared. "Ain't you innocent? Everybody makes a will whether they've got anything to leave or not. And then how do we know she 'adn't got anything? I don't believe he gets paid all that for those drorings of his."

"All what?"

"What this house costs to run. I know it's the Back of Beyond, but there's rates and taxes, and nurses don't come for love," She chuckled, rather a horrid sound, I thought. "Mind you, I don't say this one wouldn't . . ."

"That'll do, Mrs Hutchinson." I slammed the drawer of the sideboard. "I really cannot continue this conversation. It's impertinent to be discussing our employer's affairs.''

She trailed after me, draping herself against the jamb of the door.

"I do dislike ingratitood," she observed. "I'm only warning you, Mrs Merton.''

"Warning me against what?" I was almost at the end of my tether. "If you are suggesting that Mr Carringford is in any way responsible for his wife's death, let me remind you that he was out of the house that evening.''

"Going into Enderton to post some proofs. I know. Well, the post goes out at seven-thirty and he wasn't back till 'alf-past nine. So he says.''

"What do you mean—so he says? I saw him myself. I happened to be in the hall.''

"It's a shame," said Mrs Hutchinson compassionately. "You being so innocent. It's like robbing a blind man. Never 'ad much to do with the police, 'ave you, dear?''

"I never had any occasion . . .'' but once again the torrent swamped me before I could finish the sentence.

"You answer this one. What was there to stop Mr Carringford coming back before 'alf-past nine and getting into her room by the French windows—she always keeps them open—and proppin' her up against her pillows and slipping out again? There wasn't no one in the place but you and Mrs Deane and both of you in the kitchen—why, you wouldn't 'ear a thing. 'Aving a nice little bit of say-so, I daresay.'' She grinned ingratiatingly.

"Even if there was a grain of truth in what you are saying," I panted, astonished at my own feelings, "what difference would it have made if he had propped her up? She might have been gasping for breath."

"Well, she wasn't gasping when you sor 'er before supper, was she? Leastways, if she was you forgot to mention it to the police. And as for propping 'er up, why, with foxglove poisoning that can be fatal."

She had my attention now at all events. "What do you mean—fatal?"

"What I say. It was in one of those books I was telling you about, only there it was a wife murdering 'er 'usband. Only thing is in that case 'e died right off. But then they did say Mrs C. didn't 'ave enough of the poison to account for 'er dying the way she did, so . . ."

I was staring at her, aghast. So that was what Nurse Cutler had meant and what she had refused to explain to me.

"Are you sure of this, Mrs Hutchinson?"

"Course I'm sure . . ."

I let her run on. I was appalled. Because it was possible.

Marcus (I found myself thinking of him like that) could have come back without being heard or seen and slipped away again.

If he had an alibi for the fatal two hours he was all right. But—had he?

I heard myself say, "In any case, I don't suppose he knew—about propping her up, I mean? I certainly didn't."

"Well, dear, you wouldn't tell the police if you did—any more than 'e would." Her eyes, as round and brown as brandy balls, never left my face.

"You say that when you sor 'er at seven o'clock

she was lying down and she was all right then, bar
the coma, of course. But after supper she was propped
up. Well, she couldn't have done it herself, not if
she was in a coma, and you know 'er. She wouldn't
have lifted a finger to 'elp 'erself. It was ring, ring,
ring all the time with her.''

That was true, too. Things began to look blacker
and blacker.

"Now the only people in the 'ouse, *so far as we
know,* was you and Mrs Deane, and you both say it
wasn't you.''

"Why on earth should I want to harm her?'' I
exploded. "You've just reminded me that you need
a motive for murder.''

Mrs Hutchinson's gaze never wavered. "Mr C.'s
a nice gentleman, ain't 'e?''

I was shocked into silence.

"Y'see, Mrs Merton, I like you, as I said before.
I wouldn't like to see you get into a mess. Say
someone is arrested it don't have to be Mr C. Say
they take Mrs Deane. Wouldn't be the first time
she's been under suspicion. Well, what 'appens? She
gets a lawyer. You know what lawyers are, twist
everything to their client's advantage. Suppose 'e sug-
gests you and Mr Carringford 'ad met somewhere
before you come 'ere?''

"It wouldn't be true,'' I exclaimed. "I never set
eyes on Mr Carringford until we met in the register
office.''

"That's what you say, dear. It's what anyone
would say. But—could you prove it? Live alone,
don't you?''

"Mrs Hutchinson,'' I told her. "I was only recently widowed . . .''

"And you've been living alone ever since? No one to keep tabs on you, I mean? Well, then, you could 'ave met 'im. 'E's always going up to London to see an editor or something. You lived in London, didn't you?"

"Do you mean to suggest that he and I—that I . . ." I couldn't take it in, I simply couldn't. What she meant, of course, was either that Marcus had come slipping in like a thief to encompass his wife's death or that we had had an agreement . . . "Why, when Nurse Cutler asked me to look in on her patient that evening I told her at once that sickroom attendance was not among my duties, and I refused to go."

"Well, dear, that's what's so suspicious. I mean, it's not natural. If you told Nurse you wouldn't give an eye to 'er invalid you 'ad your reasons. That's common-sense, same as one and one make two. Then when she was asked she could say it couldn't be you because you'd said you wouldn't go near the room."

"I went into the sick-room when Mrs Deane asked me."

"Ah, but she come, too. You was never there alone, not till afterwards."

"After what?"

"After supper. Mrs Deane come down to 'ave 'er bite and you went up to take 'er place. Go straight up, did you?"

It may sound incredible, but I found myself actually considering her—well, practically accusations—seriously. Because it was all nonsense, of course it was. I hadn't had anything to do with Mrs Carringford's death. Why should it matter to me? But in my brain a little voice said. You may be in the clear, but what about him? Doesn't *he* matter?

And the answer was he mattered more than anything in the world—beyond my own children, of course. It was ridiculous. Why, I'd only known the man about a week. And yet—and yet—oh, he mustn't be guilty, he mustn't be guilty. I couldn't endure that. I turned to Mrs Hutchinson in a fury.

"If you have no work to do," I said, "I have. I shall be glad if you'll leave me to get on with it in peace."

Mrs Hutchinson shrugged her shoulders. "Just thought I was doing you a kindness," she said. "You mark my words, there's going to be a murder trial here, and you don't want to find *yourself* in the dock."

"There isn't the remotest possibility . . ."

"Well, I dunno. Mind you, I never poisoned anyone, but you do spend a lot of time in the garden, don't you? I've seen you myself more than once down where the foxgloves grow."

"Do you imagine one can just drop a handful of foxglove petals into a dish and kill someone you don't like?" I demanded, pale with fury. "I don't know much about it, but I imagine that any poisonous concoction would need cooking up . . ."

I stopped dead. "I see. You mean, I am in charge of the kitchen . . ."

"And there's not so much as a gas-ring in the 'ouse, barring the one Mr C. brought back for 'is wife's room a day or so back, and the man ain't been to fix it yet. Funny about artists," she added, "no use with their 'ands. My Bert 'ud 'ave fixed it right away. You would have thought Mr Trent . . ."

"I have asked you once to leave me alone," I said, scarcely able to control my voice, "now I tell you to go."

"Oh, I know where I'm not wanted." She laughed and then she was gone, calling, "Ta-ta. Be seeing you."

I had the horrid suspicion that she was already visualizing me in the dock. It was so absurd I oughtn't to have given it another thought. Yet I could think of nothing else.

CHAPTER VIII

Anthony Gilbert

I TRIED TO sort things out in my mind. After Philippa came down from her aunt's room we had stayed in the kitchen—oh, quite twenty minutes—talking, before we went upstairs. She had been in a state of considerable distress, and what could you make of that?

Of course, she might simply be afraid her aunt was dying and be recalling that other occasion when someone else close to her had died of poison. Her husband—had she hated him? And if so, why? In any case it was unnatural. A young man doesn't commit suicide unless there's something badly wrong, and I wondered how much she knew that she'd never chosen to tell.

Or had she deliberately kept me down there, knowing more about the effects of digitalin than I? Well, it seemed that the choice now was between Philippa Deane and some other member of the household who had come back by stealth, propped up the sick woman and got away, unnoticed. It would be so easy. The kitchen was shut off from the rest of the house, and if Philippa and I had been talking we should have heard nothing.

The grass verge came almost to the french windows, and a man (or woman) moving softly wouldn't make a sound.

Or woman? That gave me a fresh idea. Marcus wasn't the only person who had been out that evening. How about Nurse Cutler? What alibi had she?

I remembered old Mrs Hutchinson's hideous suggestion that I might be too much interested in Marcus for his wife's good—wouldn't that apply to Nurse Cutler, too? It might.

But—I was working this out like a jigsaw puzzle— even if his wife was dead what guarantee had Nurse that the widower would offer *her* marriage? I couldn't suppose she wanted him for his money, since he seemed to have so little, but suppose she had fallen for him, as they say so vulgarly nowadays?

I couldn't dismiss that as absurd because—well, look at me. And I've never regarded myself as an impressionable woman. So—and it was then that the hideous word blackmail sprang into my mind. Suppose she could persuade him to marry her on condition she kept her mouth shut?

I don't know how I got through that lunch. Afterwards I pleaded a headache and, as Philippa actually offered to do the household shopping for me, as soon as they had all gone off about their lawful occasions, I was able to settle down very comfortably in the sitting-room with a pencil and paper and begin to work out a case against each member of the household.

The case against Marcus had already been put to
me by Mrs Hutchinson. Of course, it presupposed
that he wanted to be free—why? To marry someone
else? Or just because he was sick of carrying that
unpleasant woman round his neck.

I passed on to Trent. I did not quite see where he
fitted into the household. He was partially incapaci-
tated, but he managed to get about pretty well: he
had, I supposed, a disability pension, and possibly
some money of his own as he didn't have to look for
a job.

Well, then, if his reasons weren't financial, and
there was no reason to suppose they were, why was
he here?

The only answer I could discover was Philippa
Deane. As to why she was here, I imagined it was
because she was afraid of her story following her
round, whereas here it was known.

But even if Trent was in love with Philippa, how
would it help him to poison Eleanor Carringford?

And then I saw it. Suppose Marcus was arrested
and found guilty—who would inherit his money?

The obvious answer seemed to be Trent, his
nephew, presumably his next-of-kin. Would Trent
take such a long chance? But really it wasn't so
long. Suppose Marcus didn't get arrested, Trent was
no worse off. And very likely he couldn't afford to
marry at the present time.

I threw my pencil down.

Really, I knew too little about everyone. I didn't
know what money Philippa had or where it came
from; I didn't know where Joy Barnslow fitted in.
But whether Dr Grayling was in love with Philippa
or not I was dead sure Trent was.

I remembered the day I found them together, and her cry of anguish: "I couldn't stand it again!" Of course, there was always the chance that Philippa herself would be accused, and her past would stand her in pretty poor stead. Would Trent think of that?

Ah, but I'd always heard that murderers were men (and women) of one idea. They didn't look ahead. If he resolved to poison Mrs Carringford with the intention of getting Marcus hanged, he wouldn't see more than an obstacle being removed from his path. And to an embittered young man of his experience would a life—or even two—seem particularly important?

He had so little—health gone, future gone—the only thing left to him in the maelstrom of post-war existence was this beautiful woman he so patently loved. I even began to wonder if he could have told us more about the late Mr Deane's death than had ever come to light.

But that was wasting time. It wasn't that death we were concerned about now. I moved on to the case against Philippa. This was the strongest of all—except for motive. Why should she want to poison Mrs Carringford?

I left that and thought about Joy. She had the most chance of getting the digitalin, because she was always working just where it grew: she could pick it without anyone noticing, and supposing you had to distil it—I really am a child where violent crime is concerned—she could use the little stove in the potting-shed—there was an oil-stove I'd noticed the day I found her there with Trent.

But that brought me up against another possibility. The stove in the potting-shed. Joy went off duty

after tea—any member of the household could go
down there, and I doubted whether their absence
could be noted . . .

I came to the conclusion that nature had never intended me to be a sleuth, and I had just decided to
stop my theories, when I saw the glaring omission I
had made. I had assumed that the digitalin must have
come from the foxgloves at the foot of the garden.
But had it?

Mightn't digitalin have been used just for that
reason, that it was available to everyone?

I don't remember how long I sat there—hours I
daresay. But at last I got up and went out to the
kitchen and made myself a cup of tea, and with it
still steaming forgotten on my desk, I stared down at
my jigsaw puzzle and knew that I had found out at
last how the murder had been committed.

When a knock sounded at my door I nearly jumped
out of my skin.

"Come in," I said in a voice that didn't sound
like my own.

The door opened slowly, and there—if my guess
was right—stood Murder on the threshold.

CHAPTER IX

Christianna Brand

"HAVE A CUP of tea," said Murder, very pleasantly.

I opened my mouth to say something: and shut it again. The words wouldn't come.

I managed to speak at last. "Thank you, Nurse," I said.

The nurse.

A young woman, an attractive woman, a woman fully aware of her attractions, using them boldly, making the best of them with her short skirts and her frizzy hair-do and her nyloned legs: burying herself away out here with a long, dull case, an unrewarding, unattractive patient.

What for? What else for but for love of some man—a man first encountered, perhaps, in the hospitals and doctors' waiting rooms of Kilchester or Everdon?

As to whether Marcus had realized—by the time I had come to the end of my notes, I had known that of course he had not. No man in love, or knowing himself beloved, could have said, as he had said to me that first day in the agency's interviewing room: "Oh, Lord—I forgot the nurse."

Nurse Cutler—in love with Marcus Carringford.

Deluding herself, no doubt, that he was "too much the gentleman" to show his true feelings while his wife—a helpless invalid—still lived.

Having recourse, at last, to some small store of digitalin: the only person who might have known what I, for one, only afterwards realized—that digitalin has a taste reminiscent of strong, black tea.

Nurse Cutler, who ceaselessly made cups of tea for her patient, heavily sweetened with sugar—strong, black, Indian tea from the special caddy on the sickroom window-sill; who could easily arrange her day off to coincide with that of Dr Grayling, so that no skilled medical attention would be at hand.

She knew the ways of the house and could so easily pop back in the course of that afternoon off—entering through the french window, haul up the patient, already deep in coma, to a sitting position and leave her there—knowing, as only she would know, that in so serious a case, to raise the sufferer would accelerate death.

Nurse Cutler, murderess: who now looked smilingly into the face of meddling Mrs Merton, housekeeper, and said to me: "The pink cup is yours."

There was a scrabbling at the window.

"Oh, poor Sennacherib," she said, "I disturbed him." She went over to the window and struggled with the latch.

The tinkle of spoon in saucer seemed like thunder in my ears as I whipped out of sight the pink cup she had brought me and replaced it with the cup of tea that I had made for myself and which still stood, forgotten, pushed aside on the desk.

She heard nothing: she struggled with the catch and meanwhile Sennacherib, as is the way of cats, got bored with the whole affair and put his tail in the air and walked away. She came back and took up the blue cup of tea.

"Come on, don't let yours get cold." She sipped approvingly at her own. "I made it specially for you. To christen the new gas ring—so typical of the company to send over hot foot, when all urgent need was gone!"

I was still shaky but I sipped at my own, innocent cup. "But they couldn't install it?"

She laughed. "Oh, couldn't they? A police seal on a door that any key will open means nothing to the gas boys. 'Oh, that's only old Joe from the station at Everdon,' they said. 'That's not meant for us.' "

"But shall we need the gas ring in there now?" I said.

"It'll come in useful: I suppose the happy couple will have that room now she's gone. It's big—make a nice bed sit."

I had not realized that the marriage was quite such a certainty. "I don't quite see Mrs Deane making tasty snacks on a gas ring in a bed sit . . ."

She stared at me over the rim of the big blue cup. "Who's talking about Mrs Deane?"

"Well, you say she and Trent . . .?"

"She and Trent!" She went off into peals of crude laughter. "My dear—aren't you innocent! Philippa Deane take on that poor fellow with his cockled-up

face and his gammy arms and legs: and not a penny
to bless himself with besides.''

She gestured with her cup at mine. "Come on—
drink up.''

I fancied that she watched me narrowly while I
drank. I said: "They? Who?''

She laughed again, jeeringly. "Who? Who else do
you think has been angling after him all this time?
Poor girl—brought up all her life among sick things,
suffering things, longing to look after them, bitter
and frustrated all her life because her father won't let
her qualify as a vet herself.''

Joy Barnslow! And Trent Carringford!

She drank off the rest of her tea and added, very
off-hand but looking rather oddly into my face: "How
do you feel—quite all right?''

I did not know how long the poison would take to
work, nor what the symptoms would be. With a
vague idea, however, of pleading sickness eventu-
ally and perhaps getting away to lock myself in my
room till the others came home, I said that it did
seem suddenly very hot.

She got up and drew the curtain half across the
window to shut out the afternoon sun.

She was watching me, I thought, with increasing
anxiety. "You do feel quite well?''

"A bit muzzy," I said.

She got up out of her chair. She came close to me
and put her hand on my forehead.

Panic rose in me. I got up and backed away from
her, from the outstretched hand. "Don't touch me!''

But she came after me, she caught me by the
wrist, she hauled me back to her, and I was like a
kitten in her strong hands.

I knew then—she was no longer content to wait for me to die: she was afraid of me. I knew something or she thought I knew something, and she could not afford to wait for me to die, lest the others come back too soon and, dying, I blurt out the something she thought I knew.

Her face was terrible, thrust into mine, deathly white and glistening with sweat, under the mop of her frizzy red hair.

She lifted her terrible face and stood for a moment looking at me with eyes that seemed utterly witless, utterly mad. Pressed back into the corner, pinned in, helpless, I opened my mouth to scream, knowing though I did that there was no help anywhere near: and she flung herself forward upon me with upraised, clawing hands—and I knew no more.

CHAPTER X

Christianna Brand

WHEN I CAME to, there were voices outside the window. The nurse had me pinned into the corner still, her arm across my throat, her hand over my mouth. "Sh'h—I want to hear what they say!"

She was muttering to herself she had not heard the car: they must have come by the short cut. This was the hedged-in path that led through from the muddy lane—Dr Grayling used the lane on his route home and he must have picked up Philippa there, laden with the shopping she had been doing for me.

His first audible words confirmed as much. "I'll take it round to the kitchen."

"No, no," I prayed to myself. "Not that—not to the faraway kitchen entrance, leaving me here alone again, with *her*."

I tried to struggle, to cry out, but I was helpless in the grip of a much younger woman, used all her life to lifting, to carrying, to holding, perhaps to holding down. I could only struggle in her grasp and pray,

"Let them come to the window. Let them look in and see me here . . ."

And he did look in: but he could have seen nothing in that corner of the darkened room, for he said, reassuringly, "No, there's no one in. So sit down, Philippa, here in the sun, and let me talk to you . . ."

"Tom, please . . ."

"All right, all right, not as you and me: as doctor and patient if you like: it's for your health's sake, for your nerves."

"Don't try to persuade me again: I've decided to go."

"But Philippa, why? Why go out into the world and face it all again? You were safe here; and you had Trent."

"Ah—Trent," she said. "My dear old Trent, my 'friend and comforter'. He understands—we're two of a pair, Trent and I, normal people not treated as normal people: disfigured people, he disfigured outside, I disfigured inside."

"Philippa, why must you live on like this in the past? People don't really worry about your past."

"Don't they?" she said. "A woman whose husband committed suicide for no reason that anyone in the world could see, and who was suspected, actually suspected by the police, of murdering him."

"That was all cleared up at the inquest."

"Yes—largely thanks to your evidence. Do you think anyone believed that, Tom? Everyone knew that he was a no-good sort of person, not much loss to the world: you were our doctor, you knew both of us—don't you think that everyone said that you and all my friends had smoothed over the facts?"

"My dear," he insisted, "it was suicide."

"Yes, it was suicide. And yet, Tom—I drove him to it. I shall never feel sure that people aren't right—that I was, in a way, his murderer."

"And with this on your mind, you want to leave this one little haven of peace and security: and your dear Trent?"

"It'll be better," she said wearily. "Joy isn't happy with me here. She's jealous, she doesn't understand, she makes things difficult for all three of us."

"Don't you think the marriage will work?"

"Oh, yes," she said. "I think it's wonderful, just the thing for him. I only say that a threesome won't work. It's my fault, being what I am: there's nothing wrong with Joy—she's gold throughout, bless her heart for his sake!—solid gold."

"Solid's the word," he said.

She gave a little laugh. "You didn't always think so, Lothario."

"My dear—you've been listening to the Everdon gossips. I like solid gold as much as the next man—but not eleven stone at a time."

"I could do with a stone or two of it, now that Aunt Eleanor is dead," said Philippa, ruefully.

"Carringford wants you to stay on."

"But how can I accept? He'll be more hard-up than ever now that her little income's gone—it was a pension of some sort. How could he keep me here, useless creature that I am?"

"He kept you here before."

"No," said Philippa. "Aunt Eleanor kept us here—both Trent and me. Poor Aunt Eleanor—we couldn't love her, we didn't love her: and yet in her own odd way, I suppose, she loved us. And now she's gone—

and my poor little last hope of peace has gone with her.''

One more person off the list of those who could have wished Mrs Carringford dead: two, indeed, for with her death her husband lost, it appeared, the use of such small income as she had had.

Not that it mattered to me at that moment, not that I thought or cared about the morass of wrong judgement and misunderstanding into which my careful notes and calculations had led me—held there in the dark alcove corner, faint with the effort to struggle away from those throttling hands, to blurt out through the steel fingers that covered my mouth even some meaningless sound that might bring them, inquiring, into the darkened room.

And then, quite suddenly, she relaxed her hold. The voices ceased and in the silence her hands fell away from me and I found myself unbelievably free.

I forced my exhausted limbs to action and half hurried myself across the room to the french window. But they had gone. I heard the sound of the battered old car in the drive and Mr Carringford's voice calling out to them, and saw them turn the corner and go to meet him.

And as I fumbled desperately with the latch she was upon me again. I shook her off and stumbled over to the door: but she was there before me, leaning back against it, panting, with outstretched arms. ''Where are you going? What are you trying to do?''

''She's mad,'' I thought. Her face was terrible, white and dewed with sweat, she sagged against the door as though all strength was ebbing out of her: and suddenly screamed out at me: "It was you!"

"It was I? What do you mean?"

"It was you." She sagged against the door, her red head lolling back dreadfully against the white panelling. "*You* poisoned her!" She began to gasp, choking out her words, clawing at her throat. "The tea . . . It—was in the—tea . . ."

I stood helplessly, staring back at her. I had forgotten all thought of making my escape. "If there was poison—*you* put it there."

"I? I just brought you—brought you a cup of tea . . . Just wanted to—chat . . ."

I stood there, staring at her, staring at the two cups on the desk, the pink cup and the blue. I had changed the cups. I had switched my innocent cup for the one she had brought me: but I had not touched her cup, there was only one blue cup.

She had made that cup of tea herself, she had told me so, she had brought it down for herself and had sat drinking it: there could have been no mistake, it was true that I always chose a pink cup, and she had brought a pink cup for me.

If there had been poison in the tea—Nurse Cutler had not known of it.

And yet . . . "You—came after me."

I think the thing came in waves. Now it passed and she made a big effort, she pulled herself together, standing there braced against the panelled door. "I suddenly felt ill. I thought you looked ill, too. I just—put my hand to your head to see if it felt like mine, all clammy: and my throat was choking me."

She put her hand to her brow and suddenly I

recalled that odd gesture she had made two or three times, the shaking off of the waves of nausea.

"You got hysterical. I was only trying to—help you . . ."

She began to gasp again, clutching at her throat.

"But you held me down: you put your hand over my mouth."

"I wanted to hear what they said."

Did I fancy an echo of that leer with which she had asked me what I had seen going on in the potting shed? "I think I—passed out. I fell forward on top of you. When I came to—they were there. She was after him—I thought she was—in love with him . . ."

She reeled and gasped, horribly retching. I came to my wits.

"Anyway, you're ill. I must get help. Oh, yes—thank God, Dr Grayling's here. I'll get him."

I went over to the alcove corner and struggled to move the heavy armchair over towards her. "You must sit down, I'll go and get help . . ."

But she swayed and tottered and suddenly pitched forward, toppling, slowly and heavily, to the floor. At that moment a figure appeared at the window. He must have glanced in and seen her, for a hand in a driving glove thrust itself through the glass, shattering it to splinters, and felt for the catch: and a voice cried, horror-stricken: "My God—Estelle!"

Estelle! Who in this house called the nurse by her Christian name—Estelle?

I dodged back into the darkness behind the armchair; but he had no eyes for me, he burst his way in and flung himself on his knees beside her. "What's happened, Estelle?"

She rolled over, dreadfully heaving, so that her wet, white face stared up into his. "The tea . . ."

"The tea? My God—you've been using her tea!" Her tea.

Her special tea—Mrs Carringford's special tea, kept jealously apart in the Georgian walnut caddy on her windowsill.

I remembered how Sennacherib, the black and white cat, would be there with his chin on the caddy, asleep in the sun. I remembered how she had said, "Poor Sennacherib—I disturbed him."

Nurse Cutler had disturbed Sennacherib, going to Mrs Carringford's Georgian caddy to make herself a cup of the special tea.

She had not known that the tea was poisoned tea. *But he had known.*

CHAPTER XI

Christianna Brand

I SHOULD HAVE gone to her. God knows I have reproached myself since that I did not.

But I was stupefied, I suppose, by the shock and the pain and the terrors of the past half-hour, and all I can say now is that I crouched there, unseen and unremembered, listening in a fascination of horror and dread—and it never entered my numbed brain that there was anything else that I could do.

He knelt beside her. I could see her white face, glistening with the cold sweat, turning restlessly on the cushion that he had put under her head. "You—killed her!" she said.

"Because of you," he said, savagely. "It was your fault. Following me down here from those London days, taking this job to be near me . . ."

She mumbled something and suddenly his voice changed; he saw, I suppose, that this would be, could be, his only hope.

"I know, yes, I know you love me, Estelle: and

you won't give me away, will you? It was your fault—letting her see what there was between us—it was your fault, so you must protect me now. She hated me, Estelle: she stuck to me because there was nobody else she could turn to, but ever since that Philippa business she'd hated me.''

Philippa! Whose husband had killed himself because he had found her out in an affair with another man.

"I kept her quiet while there was no other woman in my life—she could weave a tragic romance round our loves, I suppose: but you came here, Estelle, and I couldn't keep my hands off you—and she saw.

"I thought I could end it all—it was so easy, digitalin in the tea-caddy, little doses adding up, adding up. But it didn't work, she was inoculated against the stuff, I suppose, by all she had taken medicinally. I increased the dose, I saturated the tea with it.

"I thought I could get in easily enough after she was dead—who had more chance than I?—and remove the stuff: but the police locked the room. I didn't worry much, they'd missed the tea-caddy— that Georgian thing would look like an ornament, I suppose. They probably never even tried to open it.

"I thought it was safe, locked away in there. And now—you. But we'll save you, Estelle: only you'll never tell, will you? I'll be safe with you?''

She turned her poor head on the pillow, she choked out another question. "Oh—that. You remember that afternoon, your precious afternoon out? I spoilt it, having to leave you for a little while. I came back here, Estelle: slipped through from the lane and just—sat her up.

"In a really bad case it can be fatal instantaneously."

He was silent for a long moment, looking down into her face: and then he began to talk, rapidly, carelessly, holding her attention, riveting it on him.

"It was because of Philippa, Estelle. Her husband committed suicide because he found out she was having an affair with me: and he and she were both my patients at the time. One word from Mrs Carringford to the General Medical Council—and I was ruined for ever . . ."

He gabbled on and on: and as he spoke, with one swift movement jerked her into a sitting position and held her there.

I broke through the web of my inanition and began to scramble past the big armchair: but once again, as I moved, someone appeared at the french window and stood staring, horrified, in.

He laid her back gently with her head on the cushion and lifted a white face to the face at the window. "Something terrible has happened, Carringford."

He got up and stood with reverent, bent head, looking down at her. "I'm afraid she's dead," said Dr Tom Grayling.

But all this—and the subsequent history of my evidence at the trial, of the conviction and execution of Thomas Grayling, murderer—I shall not trouble to explain to my prospective new employer, a Mr Smith.

The same agency has sent him my particulars. I am waiting now in the the little room at their offices to be interviewed. The door opens and he comes in. I stumble to my feet, clutching my handbag.

"Mr—Smith?"

He consults the agency's letter. "Mrs Merton?" He is terribly nervous, he rattles it all off like a machine-gun. "I'm looking for a housekeeper, four in family, depths of the country, no amenities, no neighbours, no shops, no children, no dogs . . ."

"But one cat?" I say.

"Well—yes. One cat." He looks at me miserably. "Even for the sake of the cat—I suppose you wouldn't take it on?"

My hands shake on the handle of my bag. "I don't think I could," I say.

"A pity. It would have been—a permanency. And your last employer gave you such excellent references . . ."

"That was very kind of him," I say, tartly. "What kind of references did your last housekeeper give *you*?"

"Not too good," he admits. "The truth is, there was a misunderstanding. I felt ill one morning and took a drop of brandy to pull myself together: I'd been through a bad time. She came in before the pulling together process had quite been accomplished.

"And later, when I offered her the—permanency— she said that she wouldn't stay with a man who drank." He gave a little, reminiscent smile. "She was a lady of exceptionally vivid imagination! But I'm afraid I resented it, and we parted."

My idiotic, middle-aged heart suddenly for no apparent reason, stands on its head. "You don't drink after all?"

"I didn't then," he says. He eyes me beadily. "But, of course, after this distressing accusation . . ."

"You mean you've taken to drinking now?"

"Like a fish," says Mr Smith cheerfully.

I make up my mind. I snap-to the fastening of my bag with a formidable click and rise to my feet. "Well, Mr Smith, I'm afraid I couldn't accept the post. I should strongly advise you to—to . . ."

I am obliged to take a moment off while my heart does another of those disconcerting somersaults.

"I should strongly advise you to take back that last housekeeper of yours. After what you've explained to me—I think you'll find she'll come."

And, leaving him flat, I march through to the inner office and up to the haughty young lady presiding at the desk.

"I'm sorry to have troubled you for nothing, but I've decided to return to the post I was in before—as a permanency. This Mr Smith, I'm afraid, wouldn't suit at all."

As he follows me through and stands at my shoulder, I lean forward confidentially.

"The truth of the matter is—I believe he drinks!"

The haughty young lady looks in horror at Mr Smith. But Mr Smith is grinning from ear to ear.